UNDER THE BLOOD MOON

Hearts on Fire

Book One

Alexis Kennedy

www.titlewavepublishing.com

Books by Alexis Kennedy

Dedicated to my mother who turned me on to vampire and werewolf movies when I was a kid.

Chapter 1

April 8, 2014
San Francisco, California

An earthquake shook the building and rattled the windows. Julia Stevens scampered out of bed, grabbing Oscar along the way, and rushed into the kitchen to hide under the table.

They both trembled in fear until it was over about twenty seconds, which felt like minutes, later. It hadn't been that strong, but it was frightening nonetheless. It was during those times that Julia was extra grateful to have Oscar by her side. He must have been grateful, too, because he licked her face before trotting back to bed. She followed right behind the dog; she had only an hour and a half yet to sleep before getting up for work.

Meanwhile, seven miles away in a hidden cavern, amber eyes slowly opened for the first time in two hundred years.

Julia tapped her fingers impatiently on the bar. Melanie always behaved this way—invite her out and then latch on to the first guy who flashed her a smile. Julia was not a prude by any means—she was all for the occasional hook-up—but at least she was picky. She flipped her long blond hair over her shoulder and downed her drink. Then she tapped her empty glass to get the cute bartender's attention—he was worth taking home. While waiting for her drink, she looked around the new club, Howl, to find

Mel or at least someone decent to look at. There were a couple of hotties on the dance floor, but they were rubbing up against their dates. Sometimes, she'd flirt with them anyway by flashing her bedroom eyes, but she wasn't feeling sexy that night. In fact, she wished she'd just stayed home; Oscar was the only company she needed.

She turned back to the bar to have one last sip before leaving when a hand casually placed itself on her ass. She turned to slap the rude individual, but her hand stopped when she turned right into a broad chest. She was in four-inch heels, standing at six feet tall, yet she was only to the pecs on the man. She looked up into a chiseled face and eyes so deep brown that they were almost black. He was a hunk for sure, but Julia liked to be in charge. She didn't like men who thought they could take liberties with her, no matter how attractive they were. She looked the hunk right in his dark eyes.

"I think you have misplaced your hand, and I suggest you remove it," she hissed.

He leaned down, giving her a nice whiff of his musky cologne, and whispered in a husky voice, "What are you going to do about it?"

"This," she said as she brought her knee up to his nuts. He stopped her, though, with a reflex faster than a cat's, and he held her bare knee, stroking it gently with his thumb.

He leaned in again and whispered, "What else you got?" He released her knee but ran his hand up her thigh until it rested on her slender waist.

"You are way too forward," she spat at him and tried to shove him away, but he was like a brick wall and didn't budge.

He grinned a sexy, mischievous grin at her and cockily replied, "I think you like it."

The truth was, she did, but she wasn't going to tell him that. She pushed his hand off her hip instead and stepped aside, causing the other to fall away too. She knew, though, if he'd wanted to keep his grasp on her, he easily could have, and she felt almost insulted that he hadn't. She grabbed her clutch and turned to leave the club, not really caring how Mel got home anymore. As she stepped away, she thought she heard a low growl, and she almost turned around to look back. *Almost.*

Chapter 2

Julia tossed and turned in her sleep; she was dreaming about the hunk. He had his hands on her hips and wouldn't let go of her. She struggled to get control, but he pulled her into his massive chest and held on tightly. He leaned in to kiss her, and though she tried to avoid his mouth, it pulled her in like a magnet and consumed her in a fiery wave of passion. She wanted to stop him, but instead, she found herself caught in an ebb tide of desire. She could feel herself growing hotter and damper with every flick of his tongue against hers, and her lacey thong clung to her and rubbed against her sensitive and swollen pink pearl.

The stranger continued to explore her mouth while his hands moved to her ass and pulled her in closer. She felt his thick rod pressing against her abdomen, and she couldn't help but want it. Her curious hand reached down to explore the size of him, and then she desperately craved it.

His throbbing heat stretched against his jeans as if it was about to rip its way out. He moved her hand away and pulled her top off while somehow also managing to remove her bra with his teeth. His hands and mouth roamed her full breasts with a fevered hunger, and she groaned when he took her puckered peaks into his hot and gifted mouth.

Julia felt like she was about to explode into tiny pieces if she didn't have him inside her soon. She dug her nails into his massive shoulders, and he answered her by yanking her panties down and slipping a finger into her warm, wet cleft. She screamed with pleasure as he moved his fingers through her petals and stroked her swollen bud with a talented thumb. Then she screamed again, when he put a finger inside her hot passage.

Clutching his bare chest and digging her nails in deeper, she begged him, "Take me," on a breathless whisper.

Her dream lover picked her up and carried her to her bed. At least she thought it was her bed; the room was too dark, and she couldn't be sure. She could see him, though, and his perfect lips were heading for hers once again. As he moved in, she stared into the dark depths of his eyes, which seemed to have gold flecks dancing in them like stars. They were strange but very alluring. Her own eyes rolled back as a thick finger again plunged itself deep inside her hot, wet center. She felt herself convulse around it as it moved in and out of her with perfect dexterity, causing another flood of her essence.

"You're so wet for me," he told her in a low, ravenous growl. "You want more, don't you?" he taunted her.

"Yes, oh yes," she replied in a husky voice hazed by her passion. Slowly he began to move down her body, planting a path of scorching kisses along the way. She felt his nails raking their way down her back, and then, suddenly, he kicked her.

Julia's eyes flew open. Oscar was chasing rabbits in his sleep again and kicking her in the back. "Get off," she grumbled and shoved him over.

Disgusted by being woken up at such an inopportune moment, she lay there frustrated for thirty minutes before falling back to sleep. No more pleasurable dreams came to her, though.

Chapter 3

April 9, 2014

Julia couldn't concentrate at work the next day. Her mind took her back to the mysterious stranger and her dream each time she tried to compile the accounting firm's budget. She saw his enticing eyes instead of the numbers on the pages before her. Finally, she gave up and told her assistant good-bye for the day. She headed home and masturbated twice.

Around 7:30, she headed back to Howl. She didn't see her mysterious stranger, but she did see Melanie in the arms of a cute Hispanic. She returned Mel's wave; apparently, she got home—or to someone's home—the night before just fine. As she watched the couple dance, she almost felt envious. It had been a long time since she'd felt a man pressed against her like that. Well, it had been a week or two.

An hour went by, and there was still no sign of him. She was just about to give up and go home when a familiar musky scent floated over to her. She looked to her left first but didn't see him, so she turned her head to her right, and there he was. He was standing in a dark corner and staring right at her. She quickly looked back down at her drink; she didn't want him to think she had been looking for him. Suddenly, she could smell the musk, and she knew he was there beside her. She could feel the heat radiating off his towering presence, and it made tingles run down her spine.

"You came back to me," the stranger declared with amusement in his voice.

She looked up into his eyes, which were amber flecked after all, and haughtily replied, "You flatter yourself; I came in for a drink."

"Your glass has been empty for at least thirty minutes. You could have left by now if you wanted to," he observed with a smug grin. "Dance with me."

Julia looked up at him; he was even taller than before since she wasn't wearing high heels. She guessed him to be at least six-foot-five, and that was a big turn on for her.

"Who are you?" she whispered with an arched brow.

"I'm Seth, Julia. It's nice to formerly meet you," he answered with an easy smile.

Surprised, she could barely stammer out, "How-how do you know my name?"

He gave a low chuckle. "I asked. Now, let's dance. I like this music." He held up his arm for her.

Curious about the large man, she took his meaty arm and let him lead her onto the dance floor just in time for a slow song. She put her hands up on his shoulders as his wrapped around her waist. She looked up at him and studied his features, wondering why she let him be in control. He was being a gentleman at that moment, but he hadn't been one the night before.

He's probably just another wolf in sheep's clothing.

Chapter 4

Julia was surprised at how well Seth could dance. He was very lithe and easily matched her own graceful moves. She had to admit, to herself only, that it felt good to be pressed against him during the slow songs—just like in her dream.

She stared up at him out of curiosity. There was something about him—something raw and powerful—and it made her desire to know him better.

"Where are you from? I've never seen you around before," she questioned.

He looked down at her and lightly touched her cheek. "Nowhere special. I've lived just about everywhere."

Hmmm...that really doesn't answer my question. "Okay, well, what do you do?"

He gazed into her eyes and played with a strand of her hair. "You're very beautiful, you know? You must be a model or actress, right?"

Julia chuckled at his assessment. "Hardly. I'm just a boring accountant; I'm a partner in a local firm."

"That sounds nice"—he looked around them at the other couples—"Listen, I have to get going, but I look forward to seeing you again." He leaned down to plant a soft, sensual kiss on her lips. Then he left her there on the dance floor with her mouth gaping.

"Hey, who's the hunk?" Melanie asked as she ran up to her.

Julia thought about it for a moment; she really didn't know. He didn't tell her his last name, and he dodged her questions about what he did for a living and where he was from.

She looked at her friend and sighed, "I'm not sure."

"Huh…I would like to take a bite out of him; you're one lucky bitch. Well, gotta get back to Juan. He's taking me to dinner." She, too, took off and left Julia standing alone in the same spot. She decided it was time to go home.

Julia fished in her purse for her car keys, having no idea that she was being watched. Yellow eyes scrutinized her from the shadows of the trees and the night. Then they looked up at the cloudless sky. There was a quarter moon that night, and the blood moon was on its way. That didn't give him much time.

Chapter 5

The night was thick with fog, and the chill in the air made her shiver. It was deathly quiet, and she could only make out shapes that she hoped were trees; she knew she was lost.

Suddenly, she heard a whisper on the fog. "Julia," someone called to her. "Julia, I'm here for you."

She thought she saw a shape moving toward her, so she turned and tried to run, but her legs were frozen. She opened her mouth to scream for help, but nothing came out, and the massive shape was right in front of her. She put her hands up in self-defense, but warm, strong hands unexpectedly grasped her arms and pulled her into a tight embrace. Soft, sensual lips took hers captive and drowned her in a passionate kiss. It was Seth.

Julia struggled to break away from his kiss. "What are you doing here, and where are we?" she gasped.

He murmured in a deep, seductive voice, "It doesn't matter." Before she could ask more questions, he plunged his tongue back inside her mouth and silenced her.

Julia pummeled a fist against his concrete chest, and he finally set her mouth free. "You didn't answer my question. You haven't answered any of them. Who are you?" she barked.

He planted blazing kisses on her delicate neck while whispering to her, "I'm your fantasy lover, Julia." Then he pulled her nightgown up and over her body.

I'm in the woods in my nightgown? Odd that she didn't feel cold anymore, despite being naked. She did feel shy, though, and not in control of the situation, which she didn't appreciate. Julia liked to be in control in every part of her life.

Just as she was about to protest, she felt his naked body and his thick, swollen shaft pressed against her. Then his hand was on top of hers while his other grasped her bare ass. He put her hand on his steely rod and guided it up and down his length in slow, steady strokes. He was huge, and it made her shamefully grow wet.

Julia found herself enjoying the feel of him and took over, playfully teasing his thick tip with its lubrication, moving her thumb around it in slow circles. He groaned in pleasure and drew a rosy tip into his mouth. When he nipped her gently, she saw an explosion of stars behind her eyes, and she squealed with delight while pulling fistfuls of his thick hair.

"Mmm…feisty. I like that," he growled sensually.

He took her hands and gently guided her down to her knees and then onto her back on the soft grass. He planted sultry kisses down the length of her slim abdomen and flicked his tongue in her navel. His heated trail continued over her hip and down her quivering thigh. Then he stopped and looked up at her, taunting, "Shall I continue?"

"Yes, don't stop," she pleaded. "I want you to keep tormenting me."

With a sexy chuckle, his mouth went back to work on her inner thigh and burned a path of desire up to her nest of damp curls.

Then she woke up.

"Oh, fuck," she groaned into the dark room. Oscar stirred from his sleep and looked over at her from his spot on the bed. She looked at her alarm clock; it was 3:00 am, and she was extremely aroused. She tried to fall right back to sleep, but Oscar whimpered at her. "Now?" she grumbled at him. "You have to go potty now?"

She rolled herself out of bed and got dressed. Then Oscar bounced right behind her through the dark apartment toward the front door. "Come on," she moaned as she fastened his leash.

A blanket of thick fog enveloped her when she stepped outside, and a chill ran down her spine. She led the dog across the lawn and once again wished that she had a house with a fenced-in yard.

"Just go already," she chastised him when he was picking out his spot. "You're too picky, Oscar."

The dog sniffed around a little more before finally settling on a sapling. While he did his business, Julia looked around the foggy darkness. She didn't like being outside in the middle of the night due to a high crime rate in the city, and the fog only made it creepier.

Suddenly, a loud howl pierced the night and sent uncontrollable shivers through her body. Oscar whimpered and sidled up to her, sensing her unease and experiencing his own.

"Come on Oscar, let's go," she ushered him. She ran to get back inside the building—that was the scariest sound she'd ever heard, and it sounded close by.

Chapter 6

Seth, king of the Lycans, had woken up a couple of nights ago—two hundred years after the vampire king had a witch curse him. He woke up hungry for food, for a mate, and, most of all, for revenge.

After he'd immediately consumed a couple of large bucks for dinner, he'd decided it was time to find civilization and figure out where and when he was. He'd been fortunate to come across a hunter who wasn't quite so lucky. He'd dispatched of the man with one swipe of his long, razor-sharp claws across the man's throat. Then he'd allowed his body to shift back to his human form and put on the dead man's clothes, grateful that they fit his tall frame.

Seth had then made his way through the woods to the closest area populated by humans and stumbled backward when he saw it. The changes were overwhelming. He'd quickly grasped the pendant he wore. It was the pendant of λύκος and his rightful badge as king. It possessed magical powers, which he'd tapped into by chanting a spell in his native Romanian language to wake it up. He'd begged it to show him what had happened to his clan. The vision he'd seen and relived caused him fall to his knees. He'd been recollecting the fierce battle between his clan and the vampires; the vampire king had had the witch curse him into a coma, and then he'd entombed him while his clan was slaughtered. Without the pendant, he would've died, but it had saved him until the time came when retribution could be paid. That time was finally upon him.

Seth had chanted again to keep the visions going, so he could see all that had changed in the world in those two hundred years. Seeing the transformations had made him tremor, but it had also prepared him to blend in. *Then he'd met the lovely woman, and she consumed his thoughts ever since.*

Chapter 7

The sun was starting to rise, so after quickly enjoying his dinner, which consisted of a couple of cattle from a nearby dairy farm, Seth shifted and let his pendant guide him to a Gypsy. Back in his time, Gypsies and Lycans weren't considered friends, but the vampires had been a mutual enemy, and that had given them some common ground to work with. He'd find out soon enough if it still did.

When he entered the shop of Madame Viola, she said, without looking up from her counter, "I'll be right with you." When she finally looked at him and saw the pendant of λύκος, she quickly rummaged under her counter, pulled out an ancient book, and flipped its pages. Then she glanced up with admiration and bowed her head to the king of the Lycans.

"It is you; you are the cursed king of the Lycans," she whispered.

"No need for the formality," he announced and waved her up. Surprised by her gesture, though, he stared at her with an almost amused expression. "How is it we seem to be getting along better in this time?"

She mouthed his words, "in this time," but no sound actually came out as she looked at him with awe. She bravely took one of his hands in hers and clasped the amulet hanging from her neck with the other.

"The myth of your rebirth has traveled through Gypsy colonies for centuries, so how may I serve you?"

"I've seen a vision of what has happened to my clan; is it true? Were they wiped out by the vampire king's army?" He pleaded with his eyes for her to tell him he was wrong.

The Gypsy flipped more pages in her book. "Yes, the vision you had is true. The Lycans were defeated by the vampires, and the few surviving clan members dispersed into the mountains. That was the last time they were seen or heard from."

Seth was deeply troubled by her confirmation of the vision he'd had. If only he'd been able to save his clan; if only he'd avoided the witch's curse.

"I'll build a new clan then," he declared with confidence. "It'll be a bigger and stronger clan than ever before, and we will purge the world of any remaining vampires."

"Per the prophecy, you'll need your queen to carry out your plans," Madame Viola remarked while still reading from the book. "The book says to claim her by the first blood moon because that's when she'll be the most susceptive"—she looked at her wall calendar and pointed—"and there's not too much time until then, so I suggest you start looking."

Lycans were fully in tune with the phases of the moon, so he knew that only meant a matter of days. He thanked her for the information and quickly left her shop to go back out into the city to find his mate, his queen. He'd almost found Julia's den during the night while hunting, but then he'd lost the trail when her scent evaporated.

Chapter 8

April 10, 2014

Another restless three hours later, Julia got up for work. The eerie howl still rang in her ears and made her shiver. She didn't want to meet the creature that could make that sound.

She flipped on the local news while drinking her first of many cups of coffee. The reporter was talking about a missing hunter, who had been reported missing two nights ago by his friend and hunting partner. James Harvey, the missing man, had never met back up with his friend, nor had he been to work for the overnight shift the last couple of nights.

The news reporter kept talking, but Julia had tuned him out. James was a client of hers and had been for years. They'd even been lovers for a while, and when that had ended, they'd managed to remain friends. She'd just seen him a week ago, in fact, to do his taxes. He was going on about how to spend his refund, including taking her out to dinner and dancing.

She recalled why they'd stopped seeing each other; he'd wanted something serious, whereas she'd just wanted a lover—a friend with benefits. She laughed quietly to herself, thinking how some things never change. That was two years ago, and it was still how she felt about relationships. She wasn't one of those women who always dreamed of their wedding day and babies. No, not her. She had grown up watching men abuse and bully her mother. Her mother had been a weak woman—something Julia vowed to never become, and she hadn't. She was strong, independent, and always remained in control—even in the bedroom. The men who didn't like that didn't last.

That made her think of Seth and how he seemed in control the other night, even in her dreams. It also made her think, curiously, as to why it didn't really bother her. In fact, it had turned her on—at least the dreams did.

Oscar whimpered and brought her out of her daydream. "Okay, okay, I hear you," she told him while giving him a pat on his furry head.

Oscar stole her heart three years ago when she met him at the local pet store. She went in for tropical fish and left with him instead. The Golden Shepherd was the only male she allowed to be in control; in fact, he had her wrapped around his paw.

She snapped on his leash, opened the front door, and almost tripped over a vase full of purple orchids. She figured they were delivered to her by mistake and checked the envelope to see which neighbor she needed to pass them on to. However, they were indeed addressed to her. There wasn't a card inside, though, which was somewhat odd. *Oh well.* She put them inside the door and took Oscar for his walk.

It was a bright sunny day with pleasant temperatures. Oscar tugged on the leash as he assumed his normal parade around the yard. "Picky, picky, picky," she mumbled and shook her head at him. As she led him toward a row of shrubs, she heard a wolf whistle behind her. She tossed a glance over her shoulder, but no one was there. She tried to look up at the building, but the sun was in her eyes, so she shrugged it off and turned her attention back to the dog. "Come on, Ossy, and pick a spot already," she scolded him. Oscar finally settled on a spot and did his business. As they headed in, though, he suddenly stopped, turned around, and started growling. Julia was startled by his behavior; he usually didn't growl at people or even at other dogs. She looked around but didn't see anything;

however, his hair was standing on end, and he continued to growl. "Come on, boy," she said in a soothing tone and yanked on his leash. "Let's go home." Oscar obeyed, but Julia kept looking over her shoulder. She was going to wonder what that was about all day long.

Chapter 9

With the tax deadline coming up, Julia's schedule was completely booked. She was grateful for the distraction, though, since it didn't give her time to dwell on James's disappearance or her haunting dreams. She was brought back to her dreams, however, when she ran into Seth on her lunch hour.

Julia chose Starbucks for a sandwich and ran into Seth, literally. She tripped on the rug inside the front door and smacked right into him while he was standing in line. He turned around and grinned wickedly at her, and she knew her cheeks were tomato-red.

"Sorry," she mumbled while looking at the floor. Of all the people to bump into...

Seth was amused. "Fancy running into you here. Oh, wait, you ran into me," he teased her. Then he reached out, tilted her chin up, and gave her an easy smile. "Will you please join me for lunch?"

Julia blushed again and looked away. It wasn't because of his offer, but rather because she was imagining him without his shirt. *Great, get turned on in the middle of Starbucks after almost falling on your face.* After composing herself, she looked up into his dark eyes, noticing the gold flecks again. Then she quickly glanced at her watch, trying to think of an excuse. She'd had alcohol in her system both of those nights, and she didn't know if she trusted herself to be calm enough to have a casual lunch with her dream lover—it would be hard to act suave if she kept picturing him without clothes. Then again, she considered, maybe she'd finally learn more about him.

"Yes, I'll join you," she quietly relented.

Seth's smile widened—the Gypsy's vision had been correct, and he'd been exactly in the right place at the right time. "Good, I'm glad I can spend more time with you."

They were next in line to order, and he waved her in front to order first.

Julia requested a sweet tea and tuna salad on rye. Her original plan was to have chicken salad, but she figured that he wouldn't want to kiss her if she had tuna breath. Not that he was a bad kisser—he was probably too good of one.

Seth also ordered a sweet tea, just to have something in common with her, but he needed real meat, so he ordered a roast beef sandwich—rare. He saw her grimace at his selection and teased her, "What? You don't like red meat?"

She shook her head and replied, "No, not that red."

He laughed and paid the cashier. Neither Julia nor the clerk noticed that the card he used belonged to the missing man in the news, James Harvey. The cashier handed Seth their tray with a flirty smile, and he winked at her. Julia witnessed the exchange and felt a pang of jealousy.

Clearing her throat, she told him, "Meat should be cooked at a proper temperature to avoid illnesses associated with salmonella bacteria and E. coli."

Seth smiled and replied, "But it makes you big and strong."

She looked up at him and smirked, "I don't need to be *that* big." Thinking about size took her back to her dream and the fullness of his manhood, and she felt her cheeks grow hot again.

"What's the blushing all about?" he asked and winked at her while sitting down on the opposite side of the table.

"Nothing," she replied quickly and looked down at her sandwich. Suddenly it wasn't food she was hungry for. *Why am I so nervous around him?* She usually wasn't that shy.

"That's okay; you don't have to tell me. How is your day going? You must be busy since it is tax time, right?" Seth had done his research on humans in the current time, so he'd be ready for anything. He reached over to lightly touch her hand and murmured, "Let me see those beautiful blue eyes."

Julia jerked away from his touch without even thinking about it, and her hand bumped her plastic cup of tea, causing it to tumble off the table.

Seth's hand was out faster than a snake's strike and caught the cup before it even spilled one drop. "Easy now," he teased her, sensing her discomfort.

Wooing her would be more difficult than he originally thought; he'd have to study up on how to be more charming. Where he was from, you chose your mate, and she didn't ever object. He knew this wasn't true for humans, though, so he'd have to be careful not to let his inner beast take charge.

"Thanks," Julia mumbled while staring at him with curiosity. "Who are you?"

"Do you really want to know who I am?" he purred and looked deep into her eyes.

She continued to study his face. He was truly gorgeous in the daylight. Even the gold flecks in his eyes seemed brighter.

"Do you?" he pressed when she didn't answer.

Julia realized she was rudely gawking at him and tried to compose herself while looking away.

He laughed, causing her to smile impishly. "You don't have to feel shy around me. I'll tell you what you want to know. My last name, for starters, is Lupul." He saw a look of confusion on her face, so he explained, "It's Romanian. My family originated in Romania and Hungary."

Unless they'd been transformed from human to Lycan, his kind didn't have last names. Seth had been born a full-blooded Lycan; both of his parents were already Lycans, just as their parents had been. Only the pure ones had the right to be king. To blend in with the humans, though, he came up with Lupul for his surname, and it meant *wolf*.

"For a living, I took over my father's business." It was somewhat true; his father had been the king when he died, and Seth earned the title. It wasn't just passed on, though; those who wanted it had to fight to the death for it.

"Oh? What is that?" Julia asked with genuine interest.

He'd anticipated her question, and after some research, he'd come up with an answer. "I'm a corporate raider." It was the closest thing to the truth; his clan had fought for land and recruited members from other clans.

"Oh," was the only response Julia could think to come up with.

She supposed it fit him; he did have a brutal looking appearance. She looked into his gorgeous face again. Besides his mysterious eyes, he had a square jawline and a pleasant smile. His hair was cut short, and it looked soft and thick. She caught herself wondering what it would be like to run her hands through it as he laid on top of her, grinding his hips into hers as he brought them both pleasure. Then her eyes traveled to his broad shoulders, which were displayed nicely in the suit jacket he wore. She could imagine digging her nails into them while he kissed her breasts. Her legs started shifting under the table due to the tingling between her thighs.

"I have to go now. Thanks for lunch," she chirped and jumped up from the table, nearly knocking it over while trying to escape.

Seth laughed to himself. He was familiar with the expression on her face. It was a look of desire, and it wouldn't be long before she acted on it.

Chapter 10

Julia felt like a foolish teenager running away from a crush, and it made her question herself. Besides being disturbingly handsome and extremely large, what was so different about him? Why did he make her so flustered? He was just a man, and she was good with men.

She was appreciative to have back-to-back appointments for the afternoon, and it worked to keep her distracted until a bouquet of lilies showed up on her desk. A card was enclosed this time.

Please, have dinner with me at 7:00 at Red Lobster. I'd like to continue our conversation. Seth.

Julia stared at the flowers. How did he find out where she worked, and how did he know about her fondness for lilies? Suddenly, it dawned on her that the orchids left on her doorstep might also be from him, and her stomach tightened. His intensity might be too much for her, and she didn't think dinner would be a good idea. Maybe that was it—he was too intense, and she wasn't into that type. Then why did he get to her?

"Ugh," she uttered just as Brad Vaughn rapped his knuckles on her door frame.

"Tough day?" he asked in his usual easy-going manner. He was one of the other partners in the firm, and about her age, while the others were older. "It can't be too bad of a day if your boyfriend sent you flowers," he teased.

"He's not my boyfriend. He's just a guy I met in a bar." She regretted the words as soon as she spoke them.

"Oh, so you've been picking up men in bars?" he asked with a Cheshire grin. "You know Carly and I broke up, right?" He gave her a slow wink.

Actually, she did know that; however, despite that he was quite attractive, she had a policy not to dip her pen in the company ink.

"So, would you like to join me for dinner tonight?" he inquired.

"Brad, thanks for the offer, but I don't date co-workers," she mumbled.

"Well, we can discuss work, and then it won't be a date; it will be a tax-deductible meal. Hell, I'll even stick you with the check," he offered with a smirk.

Julia laughed lightly. "I don't know."

"Oh, come on. You have to eat, don't you?" he pressed.

She couldn't argue with that logic. But, then again, Seth had asked her out first. Two men in one day—was it a full moon or something?

Chapter 11

Seth anxiously glanced at his wristwatch. He'd used the Gypsy to find out what kind of flowers Julia liked, and a box of chocolates waited on the counter in James Harvey's house. He had to be careful to duck out of sight when the cops had come around looking for signs of the missing hunter. It was doubtful that they'd find the man's remains since Seth had left him in a cave, and bears inhabited that area.

He hadn't found much to work with in the man's closet for dinner attire; he'd already worn the one suit the man owned. Therefore, he went to a Big and Tall store.

The attractive sales clerk searched the racks for a suit to fit him. She was all smiles at him, and he knew she'd be an easy catch if he wanted her. Normally, he would pursue a tryst with such a lovely woman, but his sights were set elsewhere.

He picked out a blue tie to match Julia's eyes, and while he tried to find a pair of appropriate dress shoes, the sales clerk returned with a black suit and light blue dress shirt.

"This will look great on you. The dressing room is over there," she remarked and pointed to the corner of the store.

"I trust your opinion. Thank you for your help," he said with a wink and walked toward the cashier. He had an hour to get ready for his date with his future queen—at least that's what he hoped for.

Chapter 12

Julia sat at her dressing table, rolling her long blond hair up on hot curlers. She glanced at the clock on her nightstand; it was five minutes until 6:00, which gave her plenty of time to get ready, but it didn't give her enough time to decide which invitation she was accepting. She'd spent all afternoon thinking of the pros and cons of each date and even considered just staying home, but she was feeling restless.

After applying her makeup, she went to her large walk-in closet to find an outfit. The realtor had joked about the closet when Julia had moved in eight years ago. She could have rented a two-bedroom apartment, for almost the same price, and opt to have a roommate to split the bills, or she could have the one-bedroom with a humongous walk-in closet. The choice had been an easy one; she had a ton of clothes and accessories and no desire to live with anyone—besides Oscar, of course. She glanced over at him as he lay on the bed and held up a red dress and a black dress.

"What do you think, Ossy?" she cooed. Her companion cocked his head and then resumed his nap. "Well, you're no help," she commented with a playful scowl.

She examined both dresses in the full-length mirror as she held them up to her body one at a time. They were both nice, so she decided to base her decision on the shoes she would wear. That was another tough choice, but she finally decided on black strappy stilettos and, thus, the black dress.

Julia put on her black push-up bra, silk panties, and black stockings. She didn't plan on sleeping with either man, but she figured that if she felt sexy, she'd feel more in control—more like her old self. She stepped into the short black dress and zipped it up. The low-cut front nicely displayed her cleavage; she used to tease Melanie about showing too much cleavage. Julia had told her, "I show them a little bit of what they want but probably can't have." Mel had accused her of being a cock-tease—she was right.

Julia sat back down at her dressing table and took the rollers out of her hair. Coiled tendrils fell to her shoulders, and she used her fingers to gently arrange them. She was all ready to go—but where was it she was going?

Chapter 13

Driving down Oak Grove Street, Julia ran back through the pros and cons of dinner with Seth. He was gorgeous, and she did have an interest in learning more about him. There was something about him that was both drawing her in and frightening her a little at the same time, and the more she thought about it, the more curious she became.

Then there was Brad. He was attractive, funny, and they had their careers in common—but she had her rule about dating co-workers. She knew she'd have a relaxing dinner with him chatting about work, the local news, and such, but was that what she wanted—something predictable? Julia thought about Seth again; he was likely everything but predictable. But is that what she wanted? She just didn't know, but her decision would have to be made because the intersection was just ahead. She could turn left toward Red Lobster or turn right toward the Long Horn Steakhouse.

Five minutes later, she took a deep breath and stepped inside the restaurant.

Chapter 14

Brad looked at his watch. It was already after 7:00, and Julia hadn't arrived yet. He wondered if she was standing him up; maybe he'd been too pushy. For his plans to work, though, he needed to quickly make his move. If she didn't show up, he'd just have to turn things up a notch; he had a limited window to work with—Armando was depending on him. He looked at the crowd piling in the front door, and his pulse kicked up a notch when he saw her. She looked perfect.

"I was wondering if you were standing me up," he exclaimed.

Julia looked at her watch, "Oh, please. I'm only four minutes late."

"Yeah, I suppose that's not too bad for a woman," he joked.

A petite waitress showed up to seat them just then, and Julia could tell by Brad's body language that he was interested in the woman. While his ogling in front of her could be considered rude, she didn't really care. He ordered a bottle of the house red to go with their meals, and the waitress quickly returned with it and took their orders.

"So, any fascinating requests for deductions lately? I've had some crazy requests myself," he remarked after the waitress walked off.

"Yeah, I had one. A woman wanted to claim the neighbor's boy because he's always at her house," she chuckled.

"You look really beautiful tonight, by the way. That's a sexy dress you wore for our date," he complimented her.

"Thank you, but this isn't a date. It's just two co-workers enjoying a meal together," she corrected him.

"Okay, if you say so. I'll take what I can get," he responded and took a sip of his wine.

Their waitress showed up with their dinners at that moment, and she blushed a little when she served Brad his.

"I think she likes you," Julia teased him when the woman left.

"I think I like you," he responded with an exaggerated wink.

"I think you're going to flirt with everyone now that you're broken up with Carly," she said and quirked a brow at him.

"No, I'm not. I've always thought you were beautiful, sexy, smart, and funny. Shall I go on?"

"No, that's not necessary. You've flattered me enough," she replied with a red face.

She must have bruised his ego because he was quiet the rest of the meal, which just made it even more uncomfortable than his flirting. It gave her time to think, though, and she thought about the road not taken—Seth.

Chapter 15

Seth glanced at his watch for the fifteenth time; it was 7:40 and Julia hadn't shown up. It was time to leave. He rose from his seat and headed toward the front door, but a woman's voice stopped him.

"I'm sorry your date didn't show up; she's a foolish woman. I'll be happy to keep you company tonight, though, and my shift just ended," a waitress announced. She'd been watching him the whole time.

Seth looked at the cute blond and considered her offer. She was tempting, indeed, and it reminded him of the days from long ago when women begged to be with him and desperately wanted to be his queen. It would be so easy to take her somewhere and ravish her body. It would be so easy to let his inner beast out. He could see himself forgetting his mission and getting lost in her embrace—but he couldn't.

"Another time, perhaps," he told her before stepping out into the night.

He ran to the woods, stripped off the new suit he'd worn for her, and transformed into his true self. Then he looked up at the moon, which was almost half-full, and howled louder than he'd ever howled before while a single tear trickled down his muzzle.

Chapter 16

Julia was ready to call it a night with Brad. He walked her to her car and opened the door for her, but then he stopped her from getting inside.

"Wait," he said while leaning in, "I want a proper goodnight." Then he kissed her.

Most of her wanted to pull away, but there was a part—the womanly part of her—who longed to feel the touch of a man again, and she got lost in the softness, fullness, and warmth of his lips.

Just as the kiss deepened, a loud, hair-raising howl tore through the night and made them jump apart.

"What the hell was that?" Brad squawked.

Julia looked around in the darkness and replied in her own crackling voice, "I don't know, but I'm not staying to find out." She quickly climbed into her car just as a pair of yellow eyes peered through the foliage nearby.

The eyes were very displeased.

Chapter 17

Seth growled when he saw the man standing close to Julia. Was he the reason why she'd stood him up? Was he the man she'd rather be with? Well, he'd have to take care of that. He followed the man's car to a house in the woods, which helped hide him from civilization, not that it really mattered to him at that point. If necessary, he would've gladly walked down the busiest street just to rip the man limb from limb.

Something unexpected happened, though. Seth was approaching the man's car as he was climbing out of it, but something unseen—some kind of force field—stopped him. Every time he tried to lunge, he was knocked backward on his ass. There was something magical going on, and he would need to find out what it was—what was protecting the man?

Seth ducked back into the woods and headed to the Gypsy's shop; hopefully, she'd be able to tell him what was going on.

Brad clutched the talisman he wore and spun around. He'd known the Lycan was there, but he wasn't worried. As long as he was wearing his Black Dragon amulet, he was safe.

Chapter 18

Julia headed home from the restaurant. During the drive, and even after she got home, she thought about two things: the kiss with Brad and the eerie howl that sounded just like the one in the early morning hours.

The kiss had been a mistake, and work was going to be awkward for her because of it. She felt certain he would expect her to continue seeing him, and that still wasn't in her plans. As she paced her apartment, she chastised herself for letting her guard down; she shouldn't have accepted his dinner invite to begin with. That's why she didn't date co-workers, she reminded herself; there was always a fall-out.

Oscar whimpered at her, and she leaned down to pat his head, "Okay, sweet boy, let's go outside." When they were out in the yard, Julia thought about the scary howl again, so she encouraged him, "Come on, Ossy; let's make this quick."

Back inside the apartment, she picked up the local newspaper and thumbed through it to see if there were any stories about wolf sightings in the area, but she didn't find any. She did come across a blurb about the search for James Harvey. It said they would be using cadaver dogs the next morning to search deeper in the woods. Then she came across a story that would keep her up all night. Two women from her neighborhood had been found strangled with cuts across their eyes.

Julia crouched down and hugged Oscar. "You'll protect me, won't you, boy? You make me feel safe, Ossy. I sure do love you."

She turned on the TV, but *The Howling* came on, so she quickly shut it off. Thinking of howling, though, made her think about going to Howl for a drink. She was bored and still dressed up after all. Maybe Seth would be there, and she could apologize. *How mad is he?*

Chapter 19

Seth hurried to Madame Viola's shop, but it was closed. Luckily for him, though, she lived above it and heard him knocking on the door. She rushed down the adjoining stairs and let him inside.

"King Seth"—she bowed to him—"What is it you require of me this evening?"

Seth reminded her that she didn't have to be so formal, and then he explained what had happened earlier at the man's house. He wasn't quite sure how she'd respond to his confession of the planned attack. In his time, war and death were a way of survival; the struggle for power was ever-constant.

Concern crossed her face, but she didn't appear to be afraid of him. "Was he wearing a pendant or a charm?"

"I'm not sure. I didn't look that closely at him," he told her.

She dug around underneath the counter in her shop and produced some newspaper clippings. They provided coverage on two local strangled women. She handed the clippings to Seth with a deep scowl.

"What does this have to do with what happened to me?" he inquired.

Madame Viola wrung her hands nervously before holding up an amulet she wore. "This is the Gypsy evil eye. It can inflict harm on others." Then she held up a second amulet she wore. "This is a protection amulet, usually passed down in Gypsy families, that will keep its wearer safe from enemies. I believe the man you're after was wearing something like it."

"So, he is a Gypsy? What does that have to do with this?" he asked, holding up the clippings. "And why does your necklace not keep me away from you?"

"The protection amulet knows when harm is intended, and mine knows that you intend me no harm. As for those"—she pointed to the articles—"I think he may be responsible. I believe he is a Gypsy, yes, but that he uses dark Gypsy magic. Dark Gypsy magic says to cut the eyes of one's victims so that the spirits can't find them to haunt them from the other plane."

She pulled out a thick book and a star chart and then laid them on the counter. She flipped through the pages of the book with her left hand while running her right index finger down the chart. "I believe he's on a mission of his own that is tied to the blood moon and you. But I'm new to the charts, so I'm not certain of the details. I'll immediately go to the Gypsy council leaders to be sure. Please come back later tonight; I fear we need to be alert and act quickly. Whatever he's up to, it's not good. Please, come back in two hours." Madame Viola ushered him out of the shop and rushed to her car with her book and the star chart in her shaking hands.

Seth watched her leave and was even more curious about the man now. He'd not dealt with evil Gypsies before, so he really didn't know what to expect, but he knew it couldn't be good. He was especially concerned since Madame Viola thought he and the man were somehow connected. She'd mentioned the blood moon as well, which brought him back to his own mission—claiming his queen.

Seth headed to Howl to see if he could find Julia or at least her scent trail to lead him to her den. Maybe he'd surprise her by knocking on her door.

Chapter 20

Julia walked into Howl, expecting to run into an angry Seth, but he wasn't there. She found herself wondering if he'd found someone else to accompany him, and admittedly, the idea bothered her. The cute bartender from her first visit there was working again, and Julia decided it was time to act like her old self. She sat at the bar and gave him a flirtatious smile, which brought him right over to her.

"Hi, pretty lady. What can I get for you?"

"I think I'll have a piña colada," she told him with a wink.

He smiled back at her and winked. "Coming right up, beautiful."

While he was fixing her drink, Julia looked around the packed club. She didn't see Melanie there, and Seth was still nowhere to be seen either. She received some smiles from men in the crowd, but she wasn't interested in any of them.

"Are you alone tonight, or is your boyfriend going to show up again before I can make my move?" The bartender was already back with her drink.

Julia looked him straight in his green eyes and replied, "I don't have a boyfriend." Then she took a big sip of her drink. He'd put extra rum in it, and it nearly gagged her. "You sure made this strong."

"Maybe I'm trying to get you tipsy, beautiful," he murmured and grinned seductively. "So, that big guy from the other night isn't your boyfriend? He sure looked possessive of you."

Julia was starting to feel a little buzzed already. She had always been a lightweight, and she hadn't eaten that much of her dinner earlier. "No, he's not anything to me," she said casually.

Then she wondered about her statement. She wasn't sure if it was entirely true; he had been on her mind ever since she had met him, and she was definitely curious about him.

"Great. Maybe I can have a shot with you then. Can I get your number?" he asked and flashed her a big toothy smile.

"Only if I can get your name first," she answered coyly.

"Oh, yeah, of course you can. I'm Chris, and what is yours, beautiful?"

"It's nice to meet you, Chris. I'm Julia." She'd finished her drink already and was feeling nice and relaxed.

"Nice to meet you as well, Julia. How about that number?" he prodded.

"Okay," she chirped and grabbed a pen out of her purse.

She wrote her number down on a napkin, but just as she started to pass it to him, she smelled an alluring musky scent, and her eyes darted toward the door. Seth stood in the doorframe, looking more handsome than ever, and his eyes were burning a hole into the napkin that Chris was holding.

Chapter 21

Seth didn't like what he was seeing. Julia, who was a vision of beauty in the black dress she was wearing, was giving her phone number to the bartender. His first instinct was to tear off the man's hand that held it, but of course he couldn't do that in a public place. So, instead, he would have to be a gentleman and romance her—but quickly. He approached her slowly and tried to turn his scowl into a smile.

Julia relaxed a little when Seth smiled at her. Maybe he'd forgiven her for standing him up.

"You look lovely," he told her and handed her the box of chocolates. "I got these for you."

Julia's voice caught in her throat, choking off her reply. He had pain in his mysterious eyes even as he smiled at her, and he was so handsome in his suit. The thoughtful box of chocolates just made her feel more like an ass for standing him up.

"Thank you, and I'm sorry about earlier, but I didn't have your phone number to tell you I couldn't make it," she told him.

"I accept your apology, and it's my fault for not writing my number on the card. Please dance with me." He took her hand and led her to the dance floor just in time for a slow song. He slipped his arm around her slim waist and took her soft hand in his while he whispered into her ear, "You're so beautiful tonight, my flower." Then, before she could respond, he took her chin and gently tilted it up while his mouth moved down to hers. He planted a soft and sensuous kiss on her quivering lips.

Julia was already light-headed from the drink, but the kiss really made her spin. She felt soft in his arms and against his lips. She yielded to his hungry mouth and found herself wanting to explore his. Her tongue was soft against his firm one, and her body molded into his as his arm tightened around her.

"Mmm," he murmured on a low, carnal growl, "I knew you would taste delicious. Let me have more." He claimed her lips with heated passion while her hands clutched his massive shoulders. Then he moved to her neck and whispered in between kisses, "Julia, I need you. Give yourself to me."

She was hazed by the alcohol, by his kisses, by his words, and by her own burning needs. She was sure she would regret it in the morning, but that night—if only that night—she would get swept away and see how the dream ends.

Chapter 22

Seth looked at the bartender over the top of Julia's head and stared into the gawking man's eyes. The confused barkeep pulled the napkin out of his pocket, crumpled it up, and tossed it in the trash can. Seth gave him a haughty grin and then went back to exploring the depths of Julia's succulent and inviting mouth. Her soft moans of delight encouraged him, and his excitement mounted; he could feel himself growing harder with each flick of her tongue. If they weren't in public, her clothes would've already been on the floor.

Julia felt her body go up in consuming flames of desire. His kisses washed over her like tidal waves, and she was swept away by the massaging motion of his strong hands. One large hand ran through her hair while the other moved in slow circles on the small of her back. Her abdomen grew warm and heavy with lust as he stoked her inferno with an expert touch. She definitely wanted to be with him—and soon.

Seth knew she was succumbing to his charm, and he was achingly ready for her. "Are you ready to leave with me, Julia? Would you like to go somewhere private and finish this?" he taunted her.

Julia looked up at him with lust clouding her deep blue eyes. Her body was longing for his touch, her eyes were craving the sight of his naked form, which was no doubt perfect, and her ears were yearning for more of his low, sexy growls. But she wondered if it was a smart idea. Then Seth pulled her closer against his rock-hard body, and as she felt his throbbing need for her pressing up against her abdomen, all doubts went quickly out the window.

"Yes, let's go back to my place."

Chapter 23

Madame Viola rushed into the shop and up the stairs to her small apartment. She had much to tell Seth. The council had given her startling information regarding the dark Gypsy and the blood moon. They were all petrified, and there wasn't much time to stop the dark Gypsy from completing his mission. The man's objective was to bring down upon the world a calamity unlike any it had ever known. He was going to set into motion a chain of events that could very well be the beginning of the end—for all.

She expected Seth to return within the next thirty minutes, and she paced her apartment while sipping some chamomile tea to calm her rattled nerves. A car passing by on the street backfired and made her jump, causing her to spill her tea down the front of her dress. She rushed to her bathroom and removed her amulets before removing her wet clothes. She used a cold, damp cloth to wipe off her burned skin, and then she went into her bedroom to put on a clean outfit. After she stepped into the room, though, the door slammed shut behind her. Madame Viola spun around in fear and came face to face with Brad Vaughn.

"Tsk, tsk, tsk…You took off your protection amulets at the wrong time," he sneered and shook his head at her.

Madame Viola's hands flew up to cover her exposed bosom as she tried to process what was happening.

Brad laughed, "Oh, don't worry about that. That's not why I'm here."

She looked frantically around the room for something, for anything, that would save her. There had to be an amulet or a talisman or something she could use, and she had to find it fast because he was walking toward her, and she couldn't keep backing up; she was running out of room.

"What are you looking for? What else could possibly help you besides the evil eye or your protection amulet, which you carelessly left in the bathroom?" He shook his finger at her like he was chastising a child.

Out of the corner of her eye, she saw her talisman of Agnok; it had low power, but it was better than nothing. She turned and ran for it and held it up in front of herself.

Brad laughed whole-heartedly at the naive Gypsy. "Oh no, not that. I'm so scared," he mocked her.

"Who are you? What do you wa—" She didn't get to finish her sentence, though, because he had his strong hand wrapped around her throat. She struggled to fight him off, but he was too powerful.

Brad pulled a dagger out of his suit jacket, loving the panic and fear he saw in her eyes as he held it up. "I think you know who I am and what I'm all about. It's too bad you won't be around to witness it, though." He gave her a malevolent smile as he stabbed her in the stomach with the dagger. Then, as her lifeless body crumpled to the ground, he slashed her wide-open eyes.

Chapter 24

Julia sped to her apartment like a race car driver. Seth didn't make the trip easy for her, though; he was distracting her by rubbing his hand up her thigh, and then he took her hand and began to kiss up the length of her arm.

Soon, they were alone in the elevator, and Seth was taking full advantage of it. He ran one hand up under her dress and grabbed her ass while cupping her breast with the other. Her hands were exploring his body as well. She ran her hands over his muscled biceps, pecs, and rock-hard abs all the while enjoying his passionate kisses. Finally, the elevator reached the third floor, and with trembling hands, she unlocked the door to her apartment.

When they stepped inside, Oscar ran up to inspect the visitor. Strangely, however, he began to whimper and then lay down on his back in front of Seth. Julia cocked her head at the dog; he'd never behaved like that before. Maybe it was because Seth was enormous.

"Who is this?" Seth bent down to rub the dog's belly.

"This is Oscar. He's my number one buddy," she told him.

"Well, nice to meet you, Oscar. I'm going to spend some quality time with your mom." He stood back up and embraced Julia in another heated kiss. Then he picked her up and cradled her in his arms. "Where is the bedroom?"

"Down the hall and on the left," she moaned in between the kisses she was planting on his neck. "You smell good. What cologne are you wearing?"

"I'm not wearing any," he answered while he laid her down on the bed. He didn't need to wear cologne because his natural pheromones were designed to draw in females.

"Well, it works for you," she told him while waiting for his next move.

When he removed his suit jacket and dress shirt, her eyes nearly popped out of her skull. Her mouth watered as she took in the strength and tensile beauty of his exquisite musculature. His smooth bronze expanse of streamlined muscle and sinew tapered down to a taut, flat abdomen, and his arms looked like they were made of steel. He was so incredibly male, and she began to wonder if she was inadequate for him. He was boasting the sexiest body she'd ever seen, and she'd seen some good ones.

Seth approached her, and she felt her excitement growing; she couldn't wait to touch every inch of him. She pinched herself to see if she was dreaming again. He lay down beside her and started kissing her neck while a firm hand ran up her thigh. Normally, Julia would be the one making the moves, but she was enjoying letting him take the lead. Something about him being the one in control was intoxicating for her. It was an exciting change of pace. She ran her hands over his strong, sexy body and was amazed by how soft and smooth his skin was. His toned muscles rippled underneath her fingertips, and she felt the heat between her thighs grow. She rolled to her side to plant kisses on his chest and then nibbled gently on his nipples. A low growl escaped his lips, and she felt her dress being unzipped.

Seth pulled her dress down to her waist and planted kisses on her shoulders. Her skin was soft, sweet, and flushed from her state of arousal. He ached for her like never before from his own excitement, and he thought he might burst from his need. He gently cupped her breasts before reaching behind her to unclasp her bra. Then he feasted on her honey soft mounds and ripened peaks.

Julia saw explosions of light and stars behind her eyes as Seth worked his talented mouth on her. "I want you," she groaned.

That was all he needed to hear. Seth reclined her back onto the bed and pulled her dress the rest of the way down. "Very sexy," he growled. He left her silk thigh high stockings in place but slowly removed her panties while his fingertips gently grazed her womanhood. "You're stunning," he told her in a husky whisper.

Julia's eyes soaked up the sight of his narrow waist, lean hips, and long, muscular thighs when he removed his pants. When his boxers followed, she gasped. He was a superb male animal in prime condition, and her body was hot and damp for him.

Seth climbed on top of her, and in one slow stroke, their bodies became one. Rockets exploded behind her eyes when he impaled her. She moved in a perfectly matched rhythm with him as they filled the room with gasps, groans, growls, and moans of undulated ecstasy.

Julia felt her body tremble from the waves of pleasure Seth was giving her, and stars continued to burst behind her eyes with every thrust he offered. When his breathing suddenly became ragged, she dug her nails deep into his broad, muscled shoulders and rode his ripple of delight with him.

Once their breathing slowed down, the lovers fell asleep peacefully in each other's arms. Seth had totally forgotten about the man from earlier and Madame Viola.

Outside, the quarter-moon shone brightly in the sky, and an angry Brad watched Julia's building. He plotted his next move.

Chapter 25

April 11, 2014

Sunlight streamed in through Julia's bedroom window, and her eyes fluttered open. She was nestled on Seth's chest, and he was softly snoring. The previous night flooded back to her, and she felt her cheeks flush and her pulse quicken. She looked over his body at her alarm clock and saw that she was going to be late for work.

Seth woke up then and felt Julia on his bare chest. He also felt aroused again. His left arm was wrapped around her, and he grazed his hand down her back and over her bare ass. His right hand reached to stroke her breast and a rosy bud that was peeking out, causing soft moans to escape her lips.

Julia was becoming aroused and looked up at him to find his lips. She was already running late, so she figured she would just run a little later.

Seth eagerly accepted her kiss and delved his tongue into her mouth while gently rolling her onto her back. He used a finger to tease her soft pink petals, and then he dipped his finger inside her velvety passage to stroke her flames even hotter. Cries of ecstasy escaped from her, and he knew she was ready for him. He rose over her writhing body and began to slide his turgid fullness into her wet inferno. When she stretched to accommodate him, he flexed his hips in a slow and steady rhythm until he was deeply embedded inside her.

Julia was wracked with pleasure from Seth's body. Every one of his measured strokes caused her to convulse in a chain of spasms that brought her closer to her dizzying explosion into a thousand pieces. When her crowning moment burst forth, she screamed his name out into the heavy air.

The sensation of Julia's body clenching around his hard, male heat brought Seth to his own fiery, cataclysmic response, and he spilled forth inside her welcoming body.

Spent from their frantic lovemaking, the lovers rested in each other's arms while Seth lightly ran his fingertips over her body. There was something about her that was taming the beast within him; he had never cuddled after sex before. That was just one more indication that she was destined to be his queen and lover for many years to come. Now he only had to convince her.

Julia reluctantly got out of bed and headed to the shower. Seth walked Oscar for her while she cleaned up, and it was forty-five minutes later before she headed outside to her car, where he gave her a long, drugging kiss good-bye.

"Will you have lunch with me today?" he asked.

Julia considered his offer. She owed him a meal since she'd ditched him during lunch and stood him up for dinner. *Not that I haven't made it up to him in the bedroom...* "Yes, I'll meet you at 1:00 at Starbucks."

"Great," he responded with a broad smile. "I'll be there, and I won't order my sandwich rare this time," he laughed.

"Good," she giggled. "Well, I have to go, so good-bye for now, and I'll see you at lunch." She let him give her one more kiss before she got inside her car and drove away.

Neither saw who was watching them with eyes full of loathing and disdain. It was definitely a wrinkle in Brad's plans.

Seth headed into the woods to shift and then hunt. It wasn't until after he'd eaten a large buck that he remembered he was supposed to have seen Madame Viola. Being with Julia had truly distracted him, but he had no complaints about it.

He ran back to the hunter's house and changed clothes. Then he headed toward Madame Viola's shop, full of hope that she had something to report.

Chapter 26

Julia snuck into the office, but Brad cornered her in the break room. "Did someone have too much to drink last night?" he teased her.

Her face turned beet red, and she refused to make eye contact with him. "I just forgot to set my alarm," she lied. She brushed past him and practically ran back to her office.

Her administrative assistant knocked on her door. "I rescheduled your morning appointments for tomorrow morning," Marisol told her.

"Great and thank you. I appreciate you being on top of that for me. I wasn't feeling well this morning," she lied again. In truth, she felt wonderful.

The rest of the morning went by fairly slow. She couldn't help but wonder if it was because she was excited about seeing Seth again, and that made her stop and think. She didn't want to get caught up in him, or anyone for that matter, and lose her single identity. Then again, after their night and morning together, she couldn't really see herself enjoying the company of anyone else. Seth had filled her needs like no one ever had before. Sure, she'd had an abundance of great sex, but he was by far her best lover. Of course, that was just the sex. *What else do I have in common with him?*

Brad unpleasantly interrupted her thoughts. "Knock, knock. Can I come in?"

She looked up at him while mentally rolling her eyes. "If I say no, will you leave?"

"Ouch," he exclaimed and theatrically put his hand to his heart. "That hurts, and here I came by to see if you'd like to have lunch with me."

"I can't today," she told him.

"Oh, why not?" he pressed.

"I'm working through lunch to catch up on the budget plans," she lied.

"Okay, well I'll stay and help you. I've wanted to take a look at the budget anyway."

Shit. "Okay, you've caught me. I'm meeting someone for lunch," she admitted and glanced away from his stare.

"Oh-h-h, a secret lunch meeting. It must be a date then. Is this another guy you picked up in a bar?"

"Does it matter?" she inquired in a clipped tone.

"Of course not, but I thought maybe our kiss could be continued," he suggested and approached her desk.

"I don't think that's wise. I told you that I don't date co-workers," she sighed.

"Huh. So, who is the lucky guy?" he pressed.

"He's not a co-worker, and that's all you need to know. Now, please let me get back to work." She pointed toward the door, and with a heavy sigh, he left.

Her thoughts went back to Seth. *Just who is he, indeed?*

Chapter 27

Seth tried to open the door to Madame Viola's shop, but it was locked. He knocked loudly on the glass, but she didn't appear, so he went up the stairs to her apartment door and knocked again. Still, there was no answer. He turned the knob, and it wasn't locked, so he stepped inside.

"Hello, Madame Viola, are you here?" he bellowed, but he was greeted with silence.

He sniffed the air and caught the metallic scent of death. He rushed through her apartment and finally found her lifeless body in her bedroom. Despite who he was, he still cringed at the sight of the gash in her stomach and her sliced eyes. He knew it had to be the work of the dark Gypsy she'd told him about. It had to be the man he had followed, who was, disturbingly, the man he'd seen kissing Julia.

Seth was angry with himself for not being there when he was supposed to be. Not only did he not protect the kind Gypsy from her killer, but he didn't get the information she was going to give him about the blood moon and the dark Gypsy.

Now what am I supposed to do? How can I stop the dark Gypsy and claim my queen in time?

He covered Madame Viola's body with her bedspread and went back downstairs to her shop. He looked around until he found the book and star chart she'd been looking at. Before he left with them, though, he called the authorities with anonymous information about her demise. Then he went straight to the hunter's home to study the items before his lunch date with Julia. He couldn't wait to see her enchanting smile again.

Chapter 28

Seth flipped through the Gypsy's book, looking for anything useful. It mostly contained spells and chants, but there was information on their heritage as well. He started reading about the history of the tribes and stumbled across a passage stating that one day, a Gypsy would rise, and she would be the key. He wanted to find out more, but it was time to go to the restaurant for his lunch date with Julia. Thus, he marked his page in the book and headed off to Starbucks.

Seth took the trolley across the city, and at the second stop, two women got on and sat down next to him. One was an attractive redhead, and she was staring up at him. The other was a pretty brunette, and she began to stare as well.

The redhead spoke first. "Hi, handsome. I'm Beth, and this is my friend, Jennifer"—she pointed to the brunette—"Would you like to join us for lunch?"

"Thank you, ladies, but I'm seeing someone," he replied.

"Well," the brunette spoke up, "we could still have lunch and maybe make a sandwich." She batted her lashes and gave him a suggestive smile.

"I'm flattered, but as I said, I'm involved with someone," he replied dryly.

Back in his time, it was nothing for a Lycan to enjoy the physical comforts of many women; however, the women were never the ones in pursuit, they were the ones hunted and seduced. Of course, he wouldn't do that now;

he couldn't do that when he'd found his queen—if she'd have him in time.

The trolley stopped, and he hopped off. The Starbucks was on the corner, and for the first time ever, he felt nervous about being with a woman.

Chapter 29

Nervous about her lunch date, Julia walked into Starbucks. Sure, they'd already shared the most intimate of acts, but still, she didn't know that much about him—aside from the fact that he was one hell of a lover. Seth was already standing in the foyer, and he had his arms held out.

"What are you doing?" She asked, looking at him quizzically.

He replied a wicked grin, "I'm just prepared in case you fall for me again."

"Oh, ha-ha," she chuckled.

She wasn't usually in favor of public displays of affection, but she stood on her tiptoes and gave him a quick kiss. He tasted so good, and she thought about just having him for lunch.

They ordered their meals, and true to his word, Seth didn't order his meat rare. He'd just go hunting later to satisfy the beast.

When they were seated, Julia studied him; he was just so damned handsome. "So, tell me more about your family business. I Googled you, but I couldn't find anything."

He had to recall what "Googled" meant before he could answer her. "I try to remain elusive," he said with a wink. "There's not much to tell you about my family's company. It's pretty boring stuff."

It wasn't time to divulge the truth to her. She wasn't ready to handle it, and he had no idea how to go about the explanation. He looked out the window. The day was bright and sunny, and he knew the moon was almost half-full. There wasn't much time to win her love.

"Tell me about you and your family," he suggested with interest.

Julia told him briefly about her parents and her siblings. Her family lived in Colorado, where she'd grown up, so she didn't see them very often. She explained that she had moved to San Francisco eight years ago to find herself.

"Why are you still single?" he inquired.

"I don't do well in relationships. I like having my own identity," she confessed.

It was strange; she felt she could be open with him even though she'd never been that way with anyone else. Something about him drew her in and made her feel safe. Something about him made her feel like she was meant to be there, in that place, at that time, and with him.

After lunch, she gave him a long, sensual kiss before going back to work, hoping it would get her through the rest of the day. Seth stood on the sidewalk watching her drive away, but he wasn't the only one who was observing her.

Chapter 30

Brad watched the lovers kiss, feeling the tension grow in his neck and shoulders. It was only a few days before the blood moon, and he still had to find the queen destined for Armando before he woke the dark prince. He had to find the one who would pass the test, and he saw a brunette that definitely should be tested.

He confidently approached the woman, who appeared to be waiting for the trolley. He made eye contact with the pretty lady and gave her a dashing smile just as the trolley showed up. He was careful to get a seat next to her, and he quickly struck up a conversation. He could immediately tell that she was interested in him, and he fed off it. She told him her name was Clair, and she just got off her shift at the hospital, which explained the scrubs she was wearing.

"Can I interest you in a cup of coffee before you go to bed? Decaf of course," he suggested.

"Sure, but the best coffee is at my house. I hope that isn't too forward of me," she replied with a blush.

"Not at all," he assured her with a wink. *This is too easy.*

The trolley came to a stop, and he followed her off. Then it was a short walk to her yellow house. Brad looked around the woman's home; it was small and immaculate. He didn't see anything that insinuated a Gypsy heritage, though, and according to the legend, that was of the essence. A Gypsy, who was strong in power, was destined to be the bride of Armando. She was the key to the new age of the vampires.

Clair reappeared with two cups of steaming coffee. "Here you go," she chimed and offered him one. "Would you like to sit outside on the patio?"

"Sure, that would be great," he answered.

They sat outside and chit-chatted about the weather. Brad asked her about her family and her career. He also asked her what she thought about the blood moon that was approaching. She was interested in it from a religious standpoint, which really didn't tell him if she was Gypsy or not. Some Gypsies hid their race to avoid persecution. He should know; he'd been doing it himself for that same reason and also because he was a dark practitioner.

Soon, he felt bored with their conversation and decided it was time to administer the last part of the test. He stood up and approached her, and she rose from her chair too. He got right in front of her, and she smiled invitingly. Perhaps she thought he was making a move, and in a way, he was. He reached out and clasped his hand around her slender neck and began to squeeze.

"Go ahead. Protect yourself," he commanded her.

Clair's eyes bulged like a fish's, and her arms flailed wildly in the space between them. She tried to knock his hand away, but he was too strong for her, and she couldn't break his grip.

"No?" He reached into her shirt for an amulet, but nothing was there. He shook his head. "Tsk...tsk...That's too bad."

Then he squeezed the last breath out of her, and as was custom, he slashed her eyes with the small dagger he carried. He left her crumpled body on the patio and headed back to work. It was time to catch up to Julia, and he just couldn't wait to see her, even if it was to test her.

Chapter 31

Julia tried to concentrate on the numbers in front of her, so she wouldn't screw up the tax return. It proved difficult, though, since all she could think about was Seth and when they could make love again. Her thoughts went back to the feel of him, the low growls that turned her on, and even his masculine fragrance, and she felt herself becoming aroused. She was so wrapped up in her daydreams that she didn't realize Brad was standing in her office doorway. She jumped when he cleared his throat.

"Did I catch you daydreaming on the job?" he chuckled softly.

"Brad, what do you need?" she asked in an annoyed tone.

He sat down in one of the chairs in front of her desk. "I told you earlier that I would like to see the budget, and my offer to help you with it is still good."

"Thank you, but I'm working on a return at the moment. The budget will have to wait a little bit," she replied dryly.

"I can take a look at it while you're doing the return. I don't have any appointments this afternoon." *Except maybe later with you in a hotel room.*

Brad developed a crush on Julia the first time they'd met, so he wasn't sure that he wanted to test her for Armando; maybe he'd just keep her for himself. He got up and walked around her desk to lean over her shoulder.

"Where are the documents you have done so far?" he asked.

"Here," she said and pushed a neat stack of folders toward him.

She couldn't help but notice his breath on her neck, and the musk he wore filled her nostrils. It wasn't helping with the heightened state she was in, even though he didn't smell nearly as good as Seth. When he leaned in closer and nuzzled her hair aside before kissing her neck, Julia closed her eyes and enjoyed the sensation of his soft lips on her skin. When he stopped his assault, he turned her head and descended on her mouth for a deep kiss. Seth's face ran through her mind, though, so she snapped out of it. He wasn't Seth, and she wanted him to be. She abruptly pulled away and backed her chair up.

"Brad, stop it! I'm not going there with you," she yelped.

Brad backed up chuckling, "I think you just did, and I think you will again." He gave her a wink and left her office.

"What the hell is wrong with me?" she wondered aloud.

She considered calling Seth at the number he gave her, wondering if it was too soon. She didn't want to seem needy, and she didn't want to fall in love. She didn't want to be dependent on a man for anything. However, she wanted him, so she dialed his number and invited him to dinner at her house, and he happily accepted her invitation. The rest of the day went by slowly; she couldn't wait to be in his big, strong arms again.

Chapter 32

Seth hung up the phone he'd bought and learned to use. Without his magical pendant of λύχος, he wouldn't know anything about the new world. He was elated that Julia had called him to invite him over for dinner later. He began making plans; it was time to bring her closer to the truth.

He went back to the material he'd taken from Madame Viola's shop, returning to the passage he'd been reading earlier. He had been reading about the Gypsy who was the key. *But "the key" to what?* He went on to read that the Gypsies believed that when the tetrad began in 2014, a powerful Gypsy would step forth, and she would be chosen to be the queen of the dark prince who'd been sleeping for a thousand years. Seth knew what that meant; it was referencing a vampire prince he'd heard stories about. The prince would be a plague upon the world, and Seth knew that time was running out to prevent it.

He had to find the Gypsy council Madame Viola had spoken of. He needed to seek their advice. As long as he was alive, no vampires would be allowed to roam the earth. He decided to go back to Madame Viola's shop to find out how to reach the council. He looked out the window and toward the sky. Per the prophecy, he had to claim his queen before it was too late. He had three hours until his dinner with Julia, so he had time to head to the shop. He grabbed a trolley and was at the deserted shop fifteen minutes later.

The building was marked off with crime scene tape, but he broke through it and broke the lock on the front door as well. Inside, he looked around the storefront, but the police had confiscated nearly everything. Getting the information he needed was going to be more difficult than he'd thought.

He paced the small store, trying to figure out his next step, when a female shouted at him, "What are you doing here?"

Chapter 33

Brad watched Julia's office until he saw her get up to leave, probably for the restroom, and he moved quickly. He poured an elixir into her coffee and darted back to his office.

Julia sat back down at her desk a few minutes later and got back to the returns she needed to file that afternoon. She reached for her large coffee mug, desperately needing the caffeine, and quickly drank the strong brew down, burning her throat in the process. She stood up to get a refill, but her legs were wobbly, so she plopped back down. Figuring it was just low blood sugar, she rummaged through her desk drawer until she found some crackers. She ate a couple while looking at the latest return she'd been working on. The numbers began to blur, though.

Julia grabbed her desk phone and hit the button to page her administrative assistant, but Marisol didn't answer. Then she picked up her cell phone and scrolled through the address book to find her doctor's number, but everything was too fuzzy to read. A sudden knock on her door both startled her and relieved her; help had arrived. Unfortunately for her, it was Brad.

"Are you okay?" he asked with concern and walked toward her. "You don't look so good."

"Gee, thanks," she remarked with a raised eyebrow.

"You know what I mean," he replied while putting a hand to her forehead. "You don't feel feverish, but would you like me to drive you to the doctor or ER to get checked out?"

"Yes-s-s, pleassh, that'd be great," she slurred. She tried to stand up but almost fell over.

"Whoa, I've got you." Brad slipped his arm around her waist and put hers around his neck and shoulders. "Can you walk at all?"

"If you help me," she mumbled with a big yawn.

"Sure, I can do that for you, baby," he replied.

He led her through the office and to the elevator, grateful that no one was around to witness his plans in action. Before long, he was putting her limp body into the passenger seat of his car.

While driving away from the building, he asked her, "Who is your doctor, Julia?"

"Doctor Caulfield," she said in a whisper.

"Doctor Caulfield it is," he assured her. Brad didn't know where the doctor's office was, but he didn't care; he wasn't driving her to the doctor or the emergency room— he was driving to his house.

Chapter 34

Seth looked at the small elderly woman, who stared at him with disdain in her eyes.

"What are you doing here?" she repeated in a louder voice. "Are you robbing from the dead?"

The feisty woman's demeanor shocked Seth. She wasn't afraid of him at all. Dumbfounded, he replied, "No, ma'am. She was my friend, and I just want to find out who did this to her, so I came here to look for clues. Now, who are you and why are you here? You don't look like a police officer."

She looked at him skeptically. "I doubt she was friends with you, so tell me the truth. Why are you here?"

Seth found himself getting angry, and he struggled to control his temper. "I told you the truth," he replied through gritted teeth. Then he softened his tone and continued, "She was my friend, and she was helping me."

"Well, she was my friend too," she replied sternly. Then she scrutinized him. "Who are you?"

"My name is Seth, and as I said, she was helping me. Are you a Gypsy too? Are you on the council?" he wondered.

"Me? Heck no. I'm just a customer paying her respects," she said, shaking her head. "If you need to speak to a Gypsy, you'll have to go near Chinatown. Madame Viola was the only one around here."

"Thank you, and I'll be sure to check it out." He nodded appreciatively at her before leaving the shop and finding a cab. He told the driver to head to Chinatown and was informed it would be about a twenty-minute ride. That only gave him roughly an hour to spend there before he needed to be back for his dinner date with Julia. Just the thought of seeing her again got him excited.

When the cab stopped twenty-nine minutes later, Seth paid the driver and hit the pavement. He walked four blocks before he found a shop belonging to Madame Elmira, who claimed to know all and see all. *Let's hope so.*

The Gypsy looked up at him from the tarot reading she was performing for a customer. She stared into his eyes as her hand clutched her talisman, and her face blanched. She quickly said something in Chinese to the customer, who abruptly stood and left after giving Seth a long, cold look.

"It's you," Madame Elmira accused. "Viola said you'd come if something happened to her. Is she gone?"

Seth bowed his head and softly replied, "I'm afraid she is."

"Was it the dark Gypsy?" Her tone implied that she already knew it was.

"Her eyes were cut," he acknowledged.

Madame Elmira put her hands to her eyes, which were pooled with tears. "Please, lock the door."

Seth did as he was told and then took a seat at her table.

"Did Viola get to explain to you what the council discussed with her?"

"No"—he hung his head in shame—"I was there too late. I found her, but it was too late," he repeated.

Madame Elmira went to the windows and drew the blinds. "Well, we have much to discuss then"—she looked at her wall calendar—"and we have to hurry."

Seth glanced at his wristwatch, "Yes, we must hurry." He didn't want to be late for his dinner with Julia. "I'm listening, so please explain to me what this means." He placed Madame Viola's book and star chart on the table in between them.

"Prepare yourself for a mighty challenge," she warned while opening the book. "It's going to be difficult—even for the king of the Lycans."

Chapter 35

Brad looked at Julia, who was lying down on his couch and was on the verge of falling asleep. The elixir had worked well on her—maybe too well. He didn't want her to fall asleep; he just wanted her to be relaxed. He stared down at her with lust-filled eyes, and he grew thick. He would have to sample his crush before he tested her for Prince Armando. The more he stared at her, the more he knew that to be true. He sat down beside her and stroked her hair off her cheek. She looked up at him through heavy eyelids.

"Brad?" she mumbled softly.

"Yes, baby, I'm here for you," he murmured while holding her hand in between his.

"What did the doctor say? I can't remember," she pouted, and lines formed in her forehead.

"He said you're going to be fine. I just have to take loving care of you until you're better," he assured her in a soothing voice.

"Oh, okay." She looked around the room, and her eyebrows furrowed. "Where's Seth?"

Brad felt his rage grow at the mention of her lover's name. "He's not here, sweetie. I'm taking care of you because he wouldn't do it. He told me he didn't care enough for you to bother with it," he lied.

"Oh, I see," she mumbled with deep sadness in her voice. "I thought—" She stopped and blinked her eyes several times, trying to focus on Brad's face.

"You thought what, honey?" he pressed.

"I thought he'd be here." Tears formed in her blue eyes, and it added to his rage.

"Well, I'm here Julia, and I always will be. You know that, right? Haven't I proven that to you?" He firmly pressed her hand between his again.

She cocked her head slightly. "I guess so. I'm tired, so can I go to sleep now?"

"Here, drink this first." Brad handed her a cup of coconut milk. The beverage was an aphrodisiac.

Julia accepted the drink and quenched her thirst in just a couple of gulps. "I taste coconut. It's good though," she told him with a smile.

Then something peculiar happened—she felt a warmth in her stomach, and it immediately began to spread. It traveled down to her most intimate of places, and her nipples began to tingle. Urges were overwhelming her, and her legs started to restlessly shift, rubbing her thighs together. Her head was fuzzy, and a burning began in her core and extended itself throughout her body. She glanced at Brad again. He was staring intently at her.

"What's going on?" she whispered.

Brad knew the milk was taking effect, and he swooped in for a kiss.

Julia felt Brad's lips on hers, and they stoked the fire in her abdomen. Her hands reached up and ran through his thick black hair while she savored the taste of his mouth. She felt his hands on her waist, and his fingers gently pressed into her soft flesh.

"Julia, my love, you're so beautiful," he whispered through their kisses, and he meant every word of it. He'd wanted her from the day they met, and he would finally have her—all of her. He moved a hand down her thigh and then back up it on the inside, gently grazing her skin.

"Mmm…what's happening to me?" she asked him on a breathless gasp.

"We're going to make love. You want to make love to me don't you, baby?"

"Yes, take me," she replied while digging her fingers into his shoulders. *Wait!*

His shoulders didn't feel the same as before, so she hesitated and looked at his face again. *Brad?* She was confused; she thought he was Seth. She wondered what she was doing with him, and then she remembered through clouded thoughts—Seth didn't want to take care of her, but Brad did. He would make things all right; he'd promised.

Brad felt her hesitate, so he moved his hand up under her blouse and cupped her breast. He would have her. Enough with the waiting.

Julia lost herself in his fresh onslaught of kisses. He tasted so good. She felt gravity give way as her body was lifted from the sofa, and she was carried to a bedroom. Brad lay her on the large, comfortable bed and climbed on top of her. He continued his mouth play on hers while he was quickly unbuttoning her blouse. Her hands tugged at his shirt to pull it up over his head. He helped her remove it, and her nails grazed his chest and played in the coarse hair. She tried not to think about Seth's smooth chest. It was impossible, though. The ghost of him was all around her.

Brad reached behind her back and unhooked her bra. Her breasts sprung free, and he drew a taut bud into his hungry mouth.

Julia squealed with rapture as a wave of fire moved through her bosom. Her hands dug into him as she felt her skirt being tugged down. A warm and firm hand palmed circles over her mound before she felt her panties being tugged away too. She heard a zipper, and then in a swift movement, his pants and boxers were gone. He felt so good, and she burst into pieces of heaven as she felt him enter her welcoming body.

Brad guided himself into her slowly, inch by incredible inch as her velvety passage engulfed him. She felt so amazingly delectable that he thought he might explode into her with the next thrust. He slowed his pace and measured each hot glide of flesh to flesh until he felt her own ripples of pleasure hug him tightly. That was all he could handle, and he flooded her with his molten essence.

He stayed on top of her as they both filled the room with pants of bliss. There was no way he could test her for Armando now. Another would just have to do. There had to be someone else.

Chapter 36

Seth looked expectantly at Madame Elmira. "I'm listening, so please explain the dark Gypsy, the vampire prince, and their correlation to the upcoming blood moon."

"Let's start with the blood moon." She pulled out the star chart and ran her fingers over the page. "In a few days, the tetrad will begin, and while there have been tetrads before, none were like the one approaching," she declared.

Seth listened responsively. "Please, go on," he encouraged her.

She grabbed the book. "Well, our legend says that when the first full moon turns blood-red this year, the vampire prince will awaken, be dubbed king, and claim his queen, bringing about the new age of vampires. If they aren't stopped before the crest of the fourth blood moon, the world will face a cataclysm. Human life will end." She looked at him with deep concern and something else—expectation.

Chapter 37

Julia woke up in Brad's arms, so she shot up in the bed with a squawk and the blanket yanked up over her bare breasts. "What the hell is going on? Where am I?" she yelped.

Her pounding head was fuzzy. She had no idea what had happened or how she got there. She stared at him in disgust, waiting for an explanation, while he slowly opened his eyes.

"Isn't it obvious?" he asked with a smug smile. "I could show you again." He leaned over and groped her nipple underneath the covers.

She slapped his hand away with a scowl. "I'm confused, Brad. How did I get here? Why am I here? Why would we—" She couldn't even voice what they'd done.

"Well, you weren't feeling well, so I took you to the doctor. He told you to get some bed rest, and you asked me to bring you here. Then one thing led to another," he lied.

He leaned in and kissed her quivering shoulder while his hand grazed up her thigh to her downy nest of curls. He suddenly wondered if she was on birth control. If she got pregnant, he wouldn't know if it was his or the Lycan's. *Would it be a human or a mutt?*

Julia jerked back and slapped his hand away. She didn't know if his explanation was true or not because she couldn't remember anything. *What about Seth? Why would I suddenly sleep with Brad?* It just didn't make any sense to her. She'd never been a cheater before.

She looked at her watch and panicked. She was running late; she still had to get the groceries for the dinner she was making for Seth. She started to climb out of the bed, with the blanket clutched to her naked body, but Brad grabbed her arm.

"Where are you going?" he probed.

"I have to leave, Brad. This, whatever it is, was a huge mistake, and I have to go home. I shouldn't be here. I should have never come here," she screeched while yanking her arm from his grasp.

Brad pulled the sheet away and showed her his erection. "Are you sure you don't want to stay?"

She shivered from disgust. "Absolutely not."

She dressed as fast as she could and caught the first cab she saw back to the office. Her head was still pounding, and she really didn't have time to cook, so she stopped at the Olive Garden for some baked spaghetti with meatballs, salad, and garlic bread. Then she sped home and put everything into dishes and put the pasta and bread into the oven to keep them warm.

She took the fastest shower of her life and was certain to thoroughly cleanse her lady parts. She put on a red blouse and a pair of black slacks—she wanted to look nice but not sexy. After walking Oscar, she sat on the sofa and anxiously waited for Seth to arrive, all the while slut-shaming herself.

Chapter 38

The Gypsy stared into Seth's eyes. "You were woken for a reason, king of the Lycans; it was not by chance. I have seen you searching for your mate, but there is more to this than that. The Gypsy Council came together and used our collective magic to cause the earthquake that released you from your entombment. We knew you were our only chance to stop the dark prince and his army of the undead."

"I have to rebuild my army first, but is there time? I am strong, but I am just one Lycan, and I don't know where to look for others."

"There is a key to unlocking your army of Lycans. We believe the key is a Gypsy, but we don't know who she is. The book speaks of this Gypsy as the most powerful of us all. It also mentions a sinister force, though, who is after her, the key, for their own purposes. You have to get to her before the dark prince does."

"I'd have to know who she is first. Does she know about this if she is the key to it all?"

"No, she doesn't know. We feel she is either a non-practitioner, who is hiding her identity, or she doesn't even know about her true heritage—she doesn't know she has Gypsy blood. She is to be your queen if you are to raise the Lycan army."

"But I want Julia." He glanced at his watch and panicked. "Oh no! I'm running late for her dinner!" he shouted.

"Dinner pales in comparison to the fate of the world," she advised.

"Not to me," he responded in a gruff voice. "This dinner is with the one I'm falling in love with. She will be my queen."

"Is she by chance of Gypsy heritage?" Madame Elmira asked enthusiastically.

"No, I don't think so. She doesn't know who I am, or she isn't letting on that she does," he answered with a shake of his head.

"Let me consult the cards." She shuffled the tarot deck and placed a three-card spread in front of her. Then she reshuffled and tried a five-card spread and, finally, a seven-card spread.

Seth was growing impatient; he needed to leave. "What do the cards say to you?"

"I can't get a clear reading. Maybe it's because you are Lycan, or maybe the blood moon has an effect on the cards. Can you convince her to come in to the shop?" she asked and shook her head at the tarot spread with a heavy sigh.

"I don't know, but I guess I can try. I need to go to her now, but first, what about the dark Gypsy?"

Her expression was stern. "Beware the one who wears the Black Dragon amulet because he's the dark practitioner. He's well-protected by the amulet, and he'll need to be separated from it before you can even get close enough to touch him."

"What does he have to do with all of this?" he asked her. "Why is he involved?"

"He's the gate keeper for the vampire prince. He's the one searching for the prince's queen."

"Well, I think I know where to find him. I'll figure out how to get him away from the amulet even if I have to rip his head off to do it. Now, I do have to go." Anxious and nervous, he got up to leave.

"Time is running out! You only have four days left," she called out after him.

Chapter 39

Brad paced his house, lost in his thoughts. Making love to Julia had been astounding, and he couldn't wait to do it again. It was only four more days until the blood moon, and he hadn't found the bride for the dark prince yet. If he failed Armando, it would be his demise. The vampire community was watching him; they were depending on him to bring them their new king—the one chosen for the dawning age of the vampire. Then there was the matter of the Lycan to deal with too. Brad had only heard little snippets about the time when Lycans had roamed the earth, and he thought they were extinct, so he didn't know where the hell Seth had come from. He didn't know what this one wanted, besides Julia, but he would soon find out.

He used a crucible to grind up a mixture of black toadstools, dried snails, and belladonna root. He poured the powder into a bowl and added three drops of his blood. Then he combined the mixture with a glass of wine and drank it. It was the same solution he'd put into Julia's coffee, but it would have a dissimilar effect on him. It would soon put him into a powerful hypnotic trance, so he could effectively tap into his powers of dark magic.

Once he felt the effects of the drink, he got out his deck of tarot cards and shuffled them three times before laying out a seven-card spread. The cards directed him to his past, which didn't make sense; he'd never met Seth before. He looked around his bookshelves until he located the diary of Rosci, which was his family's dynasty. Something in his heritage was connected to the Lycan, and the book would explain what it was.

Chapter 40

Julia looked at the clock; Seth was fifteen minutes late. Of course, it would serve her right if he stood her up after what she had done earlier. She decided to give him ten more minutes before digging into the pasta without him. Another minute passed before there was a knock on her door. She knew it was Seth, and she began to sweat. What if he found out about her indiscretion? They hadn't discussed dating exclusively, but it still felt wrong.

She opened the door, and without a word, he embraced her and kissed her passionately, relieving some of her tension.

"I'm so sorry I'm late," he told her in between kisses.

"It's okay. I'm just glad you're here now," she replied, and she truly was.

Butterflies ran rampant inside her chest and abdomen, making her wonder, yet again, why in hell she'd slept with Brad. She still couldn't remember anything from the afternoon—it was a complete blur. Brad had said she'd been sick, but she felt fine at the moment. Even the pounding headache was gone. *Maybe it was just a bug.*

Seth's hands began to wander over her body, and while she enjoyed it immensely, she didn't feel like she could make love to him. It would be too unnerving. She gently pushed his hands away, so she didn't hurt his feelings, and pointed to the kitchen.

"Dinner is ready. Let's eat," she announced.

"All right, my beauty. You're the boss," he relented and playfully winked at her.

Seth stared at her during dinner, which made her uncomfortable. *Does he know?* "I had a boring afternoon, but how was your day?" she awkwardly asked.

"All I could think about today was you. What do you say to taking tomorrow off and spending the day with me?" he suggested. He needed to take her to Madame Elmira for a reading, and he wanted more time with her too.

"I don't know what my schedule is, but maybe Br—" She stopped herself. She didn't want to see Brad tomorrow. "Okay, let's do it," she chimed with a smile.

"Terrific! I promise we'll have lots of fun," he gushed.

After dinner, Seth helped her clear the table, all the while complimenting her cooking skills. *If he only knew...* She debated doing the dishes because she thought it might help to hold off intimacy. Instead, though, she suggested a movie; she didn't want to be a rude hostess. A rerun of *The Howling* was on.

"That looks good," Seth told her.

"Umm...okay. Sure," she relented. A scary movie wouldn't be so bad with him there. "Have you heard any strange howling lately?"

"Maybe once or twice," he replied and studied her face.

"Do you think that's odd?" she wondered.

"No, it's probably a wolf separated from its mate," he suggested casually. "Did you know that wolves mate for life?"

She cocked her head at him. "No, I didn't know that. I'm going to look in today's paper and see if there have been any wolf sightings in the area," she stated while grabbing the newspaper from the coffee table. She flipped through it quickly until she saw a story about James Harvey. The story reported that his partial remains had been found deep inside a bear cave. The cause of death was determined to be from an animal attack. "How sad," she muttered while pointing to the article. "I knew him. He was a faithful client of mine for several years. We even went out a few times." As soon as she said the words, she regretted them. She didn't need to bring up past relationships to him. She certainly didn't want to hear about any of his.

"I'm so sorry," he sighed, and he truthfully was. He only killed humans when he had to. He was a Lycan, but he wasn't like the monster in the movie they were watching. Although, the likeness was uncanny. He'd only killed the hunter to keep his identity protected. The only enemies the Lycans had were vampires, witches, and, apparently, dark Gypsies.

"There's something in those woods," she mumbled and continued flipping through the paper. She didn't find anything referencing wolf sightings, though. "Can I turn to the news real fast?" She flipped channels before he could even respond.

A story about more recent murders, which were being referred to as satanic rituals, was on. Two more women had been found murdered. The first woman had been stabbed and had her eyes slashed, while yet another had been strangled and had her eyes slashed. The first victim was Madame Viola, a local Gypsy fortune teller, who'd been discovered by an anonymous caller. The second victim mentioned was Clair Young, who was a patient care technician at Memorial Hospital, and her body had been spotted in her back yard by a neighbor.

Seth looked attentively at the television.

Julia watched his face while he stared; he seemed deeply concerned. "Did you know either of those women?"

Seth thought about lying, but there really was no point in it. "Well, I did meet Madame Viola."

"Really?" She asked in astonishment. "Do you believe in that sort of thing?"

It was the perfect time to start revealing things—slowly. "Yes, I do believe in magical things and magical beings, like Gypsies. Why, don't you?"

She laughed lightly. "No, not really. I believe in things proven by science."

"Well, what if science just doesn't see magic? That doesn't mean it doesn't exist," he pressed.

"Hmm…I don't know." She looked at him inquisitively. "You don't strike me as the type of person to believe in that kind of thing. How far do your beliefs go?"

He thought about how to answer her. "You might be surprised," he responded cryptically.

"Okay, try me." She gave him an encouraging smile.

It was time. "Well, for one thing, I believe in Gypsy magic—I like tarot readings, for example. Have you ever had one?"

"No, I've never believed in tarot readings or having my fortune told." She looked at him like he was crazy.

"Well, will you go to one with me tomorrow just for fun?" He was hopeful with a childlike grin.

"Hmm…I guess it might be fun to try, so okay," she answered with a shrug.

"Great! I know a great place in Chinatown that is perfect. Then I'll take you to lunch to thank you for the delicious dinner you made," he offered with a grin. Then he pulled her against his body and wrapped his arm snugly around her.

Julia looked down at his protective arm. She felt ashamed for fooling him with take-out food and very guilty about the reason why. "It was nothing, and you are welcome." At least it was the truth.

Seth pointed to the TV, which was turned back to the movie. "What about that? Could you believe in something like that?" His chest was tight from holding his breath, waiting for her answer.

"In werewolves? Are you crazy?" she shrieked. "The only monsters I believe in are the human kind." She gestured back to the television as if the news was still on.

"Don't worry about that monster; I'll protect you from him."

"How do you know it's a man?" she inquired and glanced up at him.

"Just a guess," he replied with a shrug. Then he wondered how he would protect her from that monster when she apparently knew him well but had no idea what he was capable of.

Chapter 41

Brad thumbed through the book of Rosci until he found the first mention of the Lycans. There was a blurb from several hundred years ago about the Gypsies uniting with the Lycans under King Dorin in a desperate attempt to defeat the vampires. At first, the information surprised Brad. Then he remembered something his mother had told him when he was very young. At the time, he'd thought it was a fairytale, but now, as he read, he realized it was actually his family's history.

The story had been about a Gypsy who'd fallen for the king of the Lycans, but he'd rejected her. The Gypsy then turned to witchcraft to try to win his love, but that didn't work either, so she united with the vampire king, King Lucian, to take down the Lycans. She'd created a potion that would put the Lycan king into a deep slumber for all eternity. She didn't want to kill him—she loved him too much to destroy him. Her plan was to revive him in the future, after his clan was slaughtered, and try to win his love once more. That was where his mother's story ended, but the book went on.

After the Lycan king had been cursed with the witch's potion, and Lucian had entombed him in the cave, the vampire king killed the witch, so she could never wake the Lycan up. Afraid for their own lives, the rest of the Rosci clan moved away and changed their name to Vaughn. The call of dark magic was strong, however, so they continued to practice it.

Brad read with great interest that the witch's name was Isis Rosci, and the Lycan King's name was Seth. *Bingo!*

Chapter 42

Julia turned to face Seth, "Are you ever going to show me where you live?"

Uh oh. What now? She knew the hunter, and since they'd dated, she'd likely been to his house. Thinking fast, he told her, "Yes, of course, but I need to clean it up first. It's a bachelor's pad after all."

"I just bet," she remarked and looked at him quizzically. "You've probably had lots of visitors in your bachelor's pad, though," she said, trying to fish for information.

"No, you'll be the first one." He looked into her eyes and maintained a straight face.

"A gorgeous hunk like you? Surely there are other women you are seeing," she prodded.

"Thank you, and while I've dated before, I haven't been with anyone in a very long time. I've been waiting for a special lady like you," he told her truthfully. *I just hope you are who I think you are—my queen.* Hopefully, he'd find out for sure when they went to see Madame Elmira.

"That's a good line. Do you use it often?" she teased.

"It's not a line"—he stroked his finger down her cheek—"You don't give yourself enough credit."

"But you hardly know me, except—" She hesitated and blushed.

"Except for how amazing you are in bed," he exclaimed, and her blush deepened. "Isn't that what tonight and tomorrow are all about—getting to know each other better on every level?"

Julia looked at him in surprise. Perhaps he wasn't a playboy, and that just made her feel even worse about what had happened with Brad earlier. If he had been seeing other women, and admitted to it, then she would have had an excuse. Maybe there was something to this beautiful man after all...

Chapter 43

Brad stopped reading for a moment, so he could process the information. His long-lost relative had been in love with Seth. *Now, how did Seth escape his entombment, and what are the implications?* For one thing, he knew, the vampire prince would punish him for allowing a Lycan to be nearby. He'd thought the creatures were extinct, but there was at least one around. He had to do something about him, but what? He didn't know how to destroy a Lycan. He went back to the book and read some more. However, he couldn't find the information he needed. Apparently, Lycans weren't meant to be a continued threat after Seth's clan had been slain.

Brad went through his bookshelves and cabinets, trying to find anything else that might have useful information, but he struck out. He paced his house, thinking about the best approach to the matter, but he came up blank. He decided to utilize a last resort, which was the help of another dark practitioner. Using Isis for inspiration, he would call upon a witch.

Brad recalled a witch whom he'd heard rumors about. Her name was Tressa Porcayo, and he'd find her house on the bluffs overlooking San Francisco Bay. He remembered hearing that she wouldn't help anyone without a payment in the form of a magical item, so he grabbed a couple of objects from his cabinets that she could choose from. Hopefully, they would be acceptable to her.

Alexis Kennedy

Her dilapidated and sinister cottage had gargoyle statues protecting the doorway as well as talismans, which he didn't recognize, hanging over the top of the stairs and from the tree in her yard. He could swear that the talismans swayed when he walked past them, even though the air was perfectly still. Filled with trepidation, he banged the heavy iron knocker on her wooden door.

Chapter 44

The Howling was over, and *Dracula 2000* was starting. Just as Julia was about to suggest they call it a night, so she could get her beauty sleep before their day of adventure, Seth pointed to the TV.

"What about vampires? Do you think they exist?" he asked her and cocked a brow.

"This again, really?" She rolled her blue eyes. "No, I don't believe in vampires; although, I have seen people in the city who seem to think that they are ones."

"Okay, I was just wondering," he sighed and let the subject drop.

She tilted her head and studied his face. He seemed disappointed with her answer. "Seth, I'm really tired. It's been a grueling day for me. Can we call it a night?"

"Yeah, if you need to." He was heartbroken. He'd been looking forward to sleeping with her in his arms, even if they didn't make love; although, admittedly, that was in his plans too. "Are you sure I can't stay and just protect you from the werewolves and vampires?" he teased.

She chuckled, "I don't think I'd get much rest then, would I?"

"Oh, eventually," he quipped and winked at her.

As much as he hated to leave, he had to respect her wishes. Human females weren't like Lycan females. The Lycan females had no boundaries to respect. They stood strong by their mates, supported them in battle, raised their cubs, and were always ready and available for mating. It was the nature of things and had been respected by all in the clan.

Never one to give in too quickly, though, Seth pulled her into his arms and kissed her with a fevered passion. His firm tongue explored her mouth with a scorching need while his hands squeezed her hips.

The intense kiss made her ache with desire, but then she remembered her afternoon at Brad's and knew she had to end it. It was definitely going to lead to sex, and there was no way she could have sex with him right then. Even she wasn't that loose. Shame flooded her, and she was sure he picked up on it because he pulled away.

"What's wrong, sweetheart? Didn't you like the kiss?" he questioned with worry in his dark eyes.

She looked up at his gorgeous, concerned face. "It was perfect, but I just can't tonight. I'm too tired and not feeling very well. I had a migraine earlier, and I can feel it coming on again."

"I'm sorry," he replied and gently stroked her face with his fingertips. Then he bent down and gave her a soft kiss. "Please call if you need me. It doesn't matter what time it is, okay?"

"Okay, Seth," she whispered and smiled up at him. "I'm glad you enjoyed dinner, and I'm looking forward to tomorrow. What time do you want to come over, or will your place be ready for me to visit you?" she probed.

He laughed, "I'll be here at 8:00 if that's okay with you."

"Sure, 8:00 is fine. Be careful driving home." She stood on her tiptoes and gave him one more quick kiss before he left.

After he was gone, she took a tired Oscar out for his last walk for the night. The lightbulb was out on the front of the building, so it was pitch-black outside. She encouraged him to do his business quickly as she scanned the enveloping shadows. All she would need right then was another howl in the night to make her jump right out of her skin and piss her pants. Maybe she shouldn't have watched a scary movie—especially one that hit so close to home.

Unexpectedly, Oscar began to growl, and his fur stood on end. Julia panicked and looked all around, but she couldn't see anything or hear anything.

"Let's go." She yanked on his leash while red eyes watched her from the blackness, and the tip of a tongue traced the tips of hungry fangs.

Chapter 45

Brad waited patiently on the doorstep, but no one answered, so he knocked again. The second knock brought about a loud shout, "What do you want?"

"My name is Brad Vaughn. I'm from the Rosci Gypsy clan, and I need your expertise," he called back.

"What *expertise* would a Gypsy need from me?" she sneered.

"It has to do with a Lycan," he yelled louder than before. His impatience was reflected in his voice.

The lock suddenly clicked, and the old, heavy wooden door creaked open. "Come inside, and we'll talk," the witch barked.

Brad was surprised that her lovely face didn't match her gruff voice. He had expected a crone. He looked around her crude house, taking in her stock of items on display. She had a few different alters set up, pentagrams drawn on the wall and floor, and various voodoo dolls, charms, and talismans all around the room. She also had a very large boa constrictor resting on a fake tree limb, and he jumped backward when he saw it.

"Does my little pet frighten you? Don't worry; he won't bite. He's my main squeeze." She went over and gave the snake a kiss on its head, making Brad cringe, so she cackled at him. "Here, sit"—she pulled out two wooden chairs—"Tell me about the Lycan. I haven't heard that word in years."

Brad recapped the story he'd read in his family's diary, and then he told her about Seth being awake.

"Oh, that could be a problem; that could be trouble," she spoke softly while her eyes scanned the room. She jumped up from her chair and hurried over to a cauldron. He watched with interest as she pulled various jars off the shelf and added ingredients to the black pot.

"Is that a magic potion that will help me?" he asked as he walked across the room to have a look.

"No, it's my supper," she remarked and gave him a sideways glance. "I don't have a potion for you, but I can help. First, however, where's my payment?"

"Oh, here it is." Brad held out his hand with three items in his palm. One was an extra evil eye he had, another was a Gypsy magic pendulum, and the last was an amulet he'd stolen from another Gypsy a few years ago.

She eyed each item before settling on the amulet. "In case I need to curse a Gypsy sometime," she smarted and winked at him.

"Now, as far as the Lycan goes, let's see why he's here in this time." She went to one of her books and flipped through its pages. "Witches and Lycans have pretty much stayed out of each other's way throughout time," she explained, "and will continue to do so if the Lycans are reborn. Now, I know that Gypsies and Lycans haven't really been the best of friends either, but what is your particular interest in this one? Why do you wish to stir up trouble?"

Brad didn't want to reveal his poker hand—the awakening of the vampire prince—just in case she would form her own agenda. "Let's just say that his presence puts a crimp in my plans. I just want to know how to get rid of him. Will a silver bullet do the trick?"

She laughed heartily, which made him feel like a fool. "Lycans are not the same thing as werewolves. They are stronger and smarter, and according to what I see in this book, the only way to kill one is to decapitate it. Of course, you'll have to get past his fangs and claws to do that. They are strong and fierce fighters, so it will be daunting. Good luck if you decide to go after him, but keep in mind, he will be resurrecting his army. What is a king without his clan after all? That would be many Lycans to destroy, so you'll need to deal with him before he can raise the others."

As he left, Brad had a lot to consider and a lot to be afraid of. *How can I pull this off without getting killed and while getting the girl?*

Tressa watched the Gypsy leave from her small window. Then she got out some potions and mixed them together while she looked more through her book. She wanted the real reason the Gypsy was interested in the Lycan, and she would find it.

Chapter 46

April 12, 2014

Julia woke up at 6:30 to the unpleasant sound of her alarm clock. At first, she lay in bed and started to mentally run down her day, like usual, but then she remembered not wanting to run into Brad at work and, more importantly, that she wasn't going to work; she was taking the day off to spend it with Seth, and that made her smile. Oscar woke up, too, and gave her a soft whine.

"Okay, baby, let's go outside." Julia got up and threw on a T-shirt and shorts. She finger-combed her messy hair, deciding it would just have to do.

Outside, the sun was rising brightly in the sky, and she had to shield her eyes from its light. Oscar was surveying the area and began to whimper. She searched the shrubs and trees to see what his fuss was about, but nothing was there.

He must be just remembering last night. "It's okay, Ossy. There's nothing there. Do your business."

He listened and quickly picked a shrub. When they got back upstairs, there was a vase of blood orchids waiting outside her door. Just like the last time, there was no card. She took them inside and set them by the kitchen sink. She didn't think they came from Seth, because he would have brought them when he showed up at 8:00. *Wouldn't he?* Unless he was surprising her, but still, he would have enclosed a card. *Right?* He'd never said anything about the other mysterious flowers, so they weren't from him. Therefore, the orchids must not be either, which made her question, "Who are they from?"

Brushing it off for the moment, she climbed into the shower. She couldn't shake the mysterious bouquet from her thoughts, though, as she lathered up. She supposed they could be from Brad, and a wave of nausea overcame her. She hoped he didn't think their encounter meant anything to her. It was just a humongous mistake. Then again, Brad came across as arrogant most of the time, so she didn't think he'd leave an unsigned card either. It made her wonder, then, if she had an admirer among her neighbors, and the thought was unsettling. She didn't like the idea of being watched.

Over the noise of the running water, Julia didn't hear Oscar growling at the front door. By the time she finished bathing, though, he was lying protectively on the bathmat with his eyes fixed on the open bathroom doorway.

Chapter 47

Seth woke up early and couldn't fall back to sleep; he was way too wound up about spending the day with Julia. Being out in public with her, as a couple, was going to be very exciting and new for him. He was eager for her to get the tarot reading, too, so he could introduce her to his world. He only had a few days left to woo her.

He groomed himself and left early for her house. He figured he could walk around the block if he was too early for her, or he could take her dog out if she hadn't done so already. When he got there, however, he tore a path around the building, removed his clothes, shifted into Lycan shape, and continued his war path through the wooded area behind her building. He didn't even care if he was seen by humans; he was on a mission to find something he'd smelled—he had smelled a vampire.

Seth searched the area thoroughly until the scent trail was gone. Then he headed back toward Julia's building and dressed again. It was time to knock on her door. He took the stairs, but he almost fell backward down them when he opened the door at the top and smelled vampire in the hallway.

Chapter 48

Brad arrived at the office early because he was hoping to run into Julia before the others came in. She wasn't there yet, though, which was odd since she was usually the first one to arrive. He noticed the answering machine blinking, and even though it was the administrative assistant's job, he pushed the play button. Julia's sweet voice came over the speaker and informed the office that she wouldn't be coming in because she didn't feel well. When the message ended, Brad jotted a note for his own administrative assistant, stating that he would be back later. Then he headed to Julia's apartment to see if she was truly sick. If she was, he'd comfort her and then possibly seduce her again—he still had some of the elixir handy. If she wasn't sick, then she would probably be with the Lycan, and he'd spy on them. It was best to know your enemy and their weaknesses before battle, and at that moment, he only knew of the one weakness for Seth—Julia. He needed to know more.

When he arrived at her apartment building, he was certain to keep out of sight; although, he wondered if he could hide his presence from a Lycan. He guessed he would find out soon enough. As he approached the building, he had the sensation of being watched, but he didn't see anyone around.

Red eyes peeked from the woods. She'd remained hidden from the Lycan and the Gypsy too. Now it was time to see if the Gypsy was doing his job correctly. His time was running out.

Chapter 49

Julia eagerly answered the door. She was excited to see Seth, and he gave her a tight hug and a kiss that was filled with an urgency that she'd never seen or felt before.

"What's wrong?" she asked. She could see worry clouding his dark eyes, and the gold flecks weren't dancing at all for her.

"Nothing," he lied. "I just missed you is all."

Oscar had been lying on his back at Seth's feet again, and he whimpered softly.

"Don't worry, Oscar," Seth cooed and bent down to scratch him on his belly. "I missed you also, pal. Have you been taking good care of my girl?"

"Your girl?" Julia repeated with her eyebrow raised.

"Well, I hope so," he chuckled and embraced her for another kiss.

She beamed at him. She somewhat liked the thought of being his girl. "Would you like some breakfast before we start our day of fun?" She looked at him expectantly.

He responded with a wicked grin full of innuendo. "I'd like to have *you* for breakfast."

She laughed, "Is that all you can think about?"

"When I'm around you, yes," he answered honestly. "So, how about it?"

Julia sighed, "You drive a hard bargain, mister." She took his hand and led him to the bedroom, where he made love to her with a fevered pitch unlike any she had ever experienced before. Something had gotten into him, and she wondered what it was.

Chapter 50

Brad ducked out of sight when Julia and the Lycan emerged from her apartment with her dog. He thought for sure he was going to be discovered when it stopped in its tracks and began to growl. It looked around and sniffed the air, and Brad quickly went back the way he came when the mutt turned in his direction.

Seth was one hundred percent on alert. He also sniffed the air, trying to catch the scent of vampire, but he didn't find the scent to be any stronger than before. He was glad that the dog could apparently smell it as well; not that it would be able to protect Julia from it. He'd already decided earlier that he wouldn't leave his queen out of his sight. He'd sleep on the floor outside her door every night if he had to.

"Easy, Oscar. It's okay, baby," Julia soothed him in a calm voice and petted his head. Then she looked at Seth. "It's strange that he's been doing that lately. He's never been like that before the past few days."

Days? Yesterday wasn't the first day a vampire had been near her? "He's just trying to protect you. He senses danger somewhere, so please don't ignore it," Seth warned.

The recent murders ran through Julia's mind. "Okay, I sure won't," she promised.

They started walking, and Oscar wanted to sniff all around the building. He definitely knew his master was in danger. The valiant dog sidled next to Julia's leg protectively and looked up at Seth with worry in his big brown eyes. Seth knelt down and gazed into them.

"Don't worry, sweet boy. I'll protect her with my life," he softly promised her pet.

"What are you two boys whispering about?" she teased.

"We're talking about how beautiful you look today," he answered with a wink.

"Well aren't you gentlemen sweet?" She smiled at them both. "Are you ready to put him inside and go on our adventure?"

"You'd better believe I am," he answered enthusiastically. He was anxious to get the proof that she was destined to be his queen. There was no room for doubt in his mind that she was the one.

Chapter 51

Zephryne followed Brad until she could corner him. He was slowly following the Lycan and its woman. She stayed close to the Gypsy, but she was sure to hang back out of sniffing range of her enemy.

"You have three days, Gypsy," she hissed when she revealed herself to Brad.

Brad jumped in surprise; the vampire scared the wits out of him. "I-I-I'm aware," he stammered out. "I'm working on it."

"Is this woman you are so intent on following the one? Is she the key for Prince Armando, or are you just chasing where your pecker points?" She nodded in the direction that the human had walked off in.

He looked down at the ground like a child being disciplined. "No, I'm not absolutely sure yet."

"Then I suggest you keep looking elsewhere, too, and do it now before I have to recruit someone else. You know what that would mean for you, right?" she threatened.

"Yes, I know," he replied solemnly.

He knew she'd kill him, and it wouldn't be an easy death either. Vampires had their ways around protective amulets and talismans, which made him wonder if Lycans did too. They'd worked the other night, but would they always? He'd be defenseless. If there was another method of protection, he needed to find it. Maybe the witch would help him again. But first, he needed to find more women to test—his life depended on it.

Chapter 52

Seth and Julia held hands on the trolley to Chinatown. She'd offered to drive, but he suggested that, since it was so nice out, walking and then taking the trolley would be more romantic. While he believed that to be true, his main reason was to be able to smell the air to see if they were being followed by the undead. If they were, it wouldn't matter who saw as he shifted and killed the monster. He was glad that it didn't come to that, though, because that wasn't how he wanted to explain himself—his race—to Julia. Knots formed in his stomach when they reached Chinatown and got off the trolley.

"So, where to?" she asked, full of eagerness.

He was glad that she was in a good mood and ready for some fun. "Well, I thought we could see the fortune teller first—her shop is just a couple of blocks away. Then I think there's going to be a parade, so we could watch that and then go to lunch. Would you like to walk or take a taxi?"

"I could use the exercise, so let's walk," she answered.

"You need more exercise after this morning?" he teased. "I can help you with that."

"Ha! I bet you can," she laughed with him.

The two blocks were a quick walk, and the bell chimed when they entered the shop of Madame Elmira.

"Good, you came back," the Gypsy said excitedly. "I'm so glad you were able to bring your lady friend. I am Madame Elmira." She rolled the *r* for effect.

"Hi, I'm Julia," she replied and extended her hand.

"Oh, I know who you are." Madame Elmira winked at her.

Julia felt even more self-conscious about being there. "Um...I've never done this before. What exactly are we going to do today?"

"Don't be nervous; it's fun," Seth assured her.

"Here, sit at the table with me," the Gypsy told her and gestured. "I'm going to use the tarot cards first to see what your future holds." She shuffled the deck and placed three cards in front of Julia. The cards were: The Hermit, Strength, and The World. "This represents your past, present, and future. I can see that you grew up with a lot of emotional pain, and you withdrew into yourself. You were afraid to let anyone else in because it could cause you more pain. In your present, I see a fire stirring inside you, which is sometimes passion, and sometimes, it is just the part of you that wants to get out—the part that desires change. In the future, you have the world. It is indicative of a complete circle. You are exactly in the place you were meant to be, and your future is full of promise. May I see your palm, please?"

Intrigued, Julia held out her hand for the Gypsy while glancing at Seth who was all smiles.

"Your lifeline shows the joining of you and another right here"—she pointed to a line on Julia's hand—"So, love is definitely in the stars for you, my dear, and since the lines remain joined, it must be your true love." She winked and let go of her hand.

"Is that all?" Julia was truly interested now.

"That's all, but please come back and visit me anytime, especially if you need charms, amulets, or pendants," Madame Elmira answered with a bright smile.

"What about children? Did you see children in my future?" Julia pressed.

"Oh, my goodness! Where is my mind today?" The Gypsy seemed flustered. "Let me have another look at your palm, please."

Julia extended her hand once more for the peculiar woman. Her mother would laugh her ass off if she knew where Julia was right now.

"Yes, I see many children in your future."

"Many? Yikes." Julia gulped.

"Don't worry, my dear, the future can always be changed"—she looked meaningfully at Seth—"In fact, I'm counting on it."

Julia looked at the woman, then at Seth, then back at the woman. "Am I supposed to know what that means?"

"No-no-no. Don't worry about things. All will be well for you. I have no doubt," she answered.

"Good to know"—she looked up at Seth—"It's your turn now," she chirped with a coy smile.

"I've already had my future told," he replied with a sly grin. "Madame Elmira told me that I was about to meet the love of my life."

"And when was that?" she wondered.

"It was the day I first met you," he sighed.

"Well, she just said the future can change. I think you need another one. My treat." She clapped her hands like a happy child.

"Oh, no, there's no charge today. No charge for the kin—" Madame Elmira caught herself. "For such a kind man like him."

"There you go, Seth, now you have to. For me?" She playfully batted her lashes at him.

"Okay, for you," he relented and sat at the table with the women.

Madame Elmira shuffled the cards again and spread out three new ones in front of Seth. Since the reading wasn't clear the last time, she didn't expect it to be then either.

The cards were: The Sun, Judgement, and The Tower. "In your past, you saw glory and triumph over your ene—" She caught herself again. "Over your obstacles. Then, after troubled times, you were reborn and resurrected into the man you are now. The future, however, shows more troubled times ahead for you. The Tower represents war. It is not always the physical kind, but rather it is often between lies and the truth. You may find that something you believe to be true is false. Now, let me see your palm."

Lies? Like me sleeping with Brad? Julia felt guilty all over again. Was he going to find out about that? She had always believed what her mom used to tell her—don't lie because the truth will come out eventually.

Seth held out his hand for the Gypsy to examine while Julia eagerly watched. "I see love in your future as well, and the love line is long. I see you meeting your soul mate and treating her like a queen." She winked at Julia.

"I know that's true," Seth replied with a devilish grin.

"So"—the Gypsy beamed at the handsome couple—"It looks like you both have a bright future to look forward to."

Seth mouthed "Gypsy?" to Madame Elmira while Julia was getting up from her seat. The woman only shrugged her shoulders in response, though.

Chapter 53

Brad followed a girl with dark hair, dark eyes, and olive skin through Chinatown. She looked Italian or Romani and was dressed in vivid colors and prints often worn by the Gypsy street performers in San Francisco. Perhaps she was one of the belly dancers he liked to watch on occasion. He watched her shop in the outdoor markets and waited until he could follow her to an isolated area, which was an alley she was cutting through—huge mistake.

The girl was surprised by his sudden appearance, and she clutched the pendant she was wearing. Unfortunately, it wasn't strong enough to ward him off while he wore the Black Dragon amulet.

He slowly approached the Gypsy girl—she appeared to be a viable candidate for his test. He chuckled when she clutched her useless crystal pendant. "Don't worry, pretty lady. I'm here to provide you with a wonderful opportunity. It's the chance of a lifetime—or several as the case may be." He chuckled at his own morbid humor.

"What do you mean?" What are you talking about?" she asked with suspicion.

"You'll soon see—one way or another," he sneered.

The girl wanted to run—she tried to run—but her legs refused to move.

Brad slowly closed in on her. He could drag things out—she wasn't going anywhere.

Chapter 54

Seth cocked his head at Madame Elmira.

"Are you coming?" Julia asked him in a pert voice. "The parade is about to start."

"You go ahead, and I'll be right there. I'm going to take care of the bill. I can't let her give us the readings for free."

"Okay, but hurry," she called out. She was already running for the door just as the drums began. Seth turned back to Madame Elmira, "Now please explain to me if she is the one. Is she the Gypsy?"

She shrugged again. "I don't know. I really can't tell."

"Is that normal?" He was totally confused and stared at her in disbelief.

"No, not really." She looked dumbfounded herself.

"Okay, so what does that mean?" he asked.

"My guess is either she's not Gypsy, or if she is the one—the strongest one of all the Gypsies—then it is her strength blocking me. Let's look at the last card again. It is about secrets that are deeply hidden, but sometimes they are hidden in plain sight."

"And that means what?" he inquired with a hint of agitation in his voice. He was tired of her being cryptic.

"It means the truth will reveal itself in time unless it already has, and you just don't see it yet."

"I feel like you are talking in circles," he snapped.

"I'm sorry. I suppose that's the Gypsy in me." They both turned to look as the Golden Dragon paraded past the door. "I think you have the answers, or truths, already.

You must look to yourself for the answers you seek. But, I've never done a reading for a Lycan before, so I cannot guarantee its accuracy. I will check with the other council members, though. Can you come back to see me tomorrow?"

"Yes, I'll come back. I know time is of the essence, and I need this puzzle solved. But, just so you know, I'm making Julia my queen no matter what. So, if she's not the Gypsy, I'll have to find another way to rebuild my army to stop the vampires."

"I don't know if you can," she warned in a worried tone.

"I will," he said while heading out the door. He looked left and then right but didn't see Julia anywhere, so he panicked.

Chapter 55

Brad brushed the girl's black hair out of her pretty face. Then, reflexively, he leaned in and kissed her. She didn't respond favorably, though. Instead, she bit his lip.

He pulled back but laughed. "I like women who are feisty, so that's okay, baby." Then he searched her eyes. "What is your name?"

"Ofelia," she answered sharply. Yes, she had spirit. But was it enough to save her? She said something in Greek that he couldn't understand and spat on him.

Hmm...I guess that was an insult. He wiped the spittle off his face. "You really shouldn't have done that, Ofelia."

He reached out and grabbed her by the throat, barely squeezing. She only flinched from it, and he couldn't decide if that angered him or turned him on. No wonder the prophecy named a Gypsy as the queen for the vampire prince—Gypsy women were strong by nature. Ofelia, apparently, was no exception.

He clutched her throat harder and ordered her, "Protect yourself."

Two surprising things happened at that moment. First off, she was able to break through her fear and bring her knee up to Brad's groin. Secondly, she sliced his side with a knife she had hidden.

Chapter 56

Seth couldn't see across the street because the Golden Dragon was still coming as far as the eye could see. He had only one option, and he really didn't want to do it in front of the large crowd of humans. However, if it meant saving Julia, he would. Just as he was ready to make his move, someone grabbed his arm. It was Madame Elmira.

"Here. Keep this with you at all times"—she handed him an amulet—"It will offer you some protection," she explained. "I just hope it's enough."

Then, while she and the crowd watched, he took one step backward and ran toward the Golden Dragon parade and leapt ten feet into the air over it.
Thinking it must be part of the parade—because what else in the world could it be—the crowd exploded in raucous applause. All, that is, except for Madame Elmira.

She shook her head and muttered under her breath, "God go with you, king of the Lycans."

She stepped back inside her shop and immediately called the other council members.

Chapter 57

Seth landed safely on the other side, and the surprised observers there also erupted into applause. He looked frantically left to right and finally spotted her haggling with a vendor over a sarong. He was incredibly relieved, but he was also livid as he ran up to her.

"Don't run off like that ever again," he growled at her.

Julia jumped from his tone. "Excuse me?" she shouted at him.

"I'm sorry," he responded softly. "I was worried sick about you when I couldn't find you. Please, don't do that again." He reached out to lightly touch her shoulder.

She pulled away, though. "Why on earth would you be worried about me? I can take of myself. I don't need a babysitter," she told him defensively. She didn't need a man to keep his eye on her and be all possessive. That's why she didn't do relationships.

"I'm not wanting to babysit you. I just want to keep you safe," he replied calmly.

Feeling a little calmer herself, she replied, "Well, don't worry about me. I'm a big girl, and I've managed just fine without your or anyone else's protection so far."

Yes, but you have no idea what you're up against. "Are you ready for lunch? I'll take you anywhere you want to go," he said, trying to change the subject.

"Yes, I'm a little hungry," she answered.

"Great. What are you in the mood for?"

Julia looked around. "How about over there at Wok Around the Block?"

"Whatever you want is fine with me," he told her agreeably.

Just as they entered the restaurant, a breeze blew past, and Seth caught a vampire's scent on it. "Stay here and grab a table. I'll be right back," he commanded before he bolted back out the door.

Confused and pissed off, Julia sat down to ponder Seth's crazy behavior.

"I see you're feeling better," Brad stated right before sitting down across from her.

Chapter 58

Tressa was still pouring over her books when the dark Gypsy dropped by again. He was holding a blood-soaked cloth over a deep gash in his side, and he wanted her to treat it for him. She quickly stitched it up and used some magical powders to assist in the healing process. He'd come to her, instead of a doctor, so the wound could be blessed while it was stitched because blessing them afterward wasn't effective. The blessing helped with a speedy recovery.

He explained to her what had happened with the Gypsy girl. "The little bitch cut me and got away. She was the first one too."

"The first one? Have you been going after Gypsies, and if so, why?" she pressed.

Realizing his slip, he clammed up tight. "It doesn't matter. I just don't like them. The good ones, of course, is what I mean," he added quickly.

"Well, I'm done here. Is there anything else? You know, I could supercharge your amulet while you are here," she offered.

He thought about taking her up on it. "Okay, why not?" Brad gave her the Black Dragon amulet he'd worn since his mother had died, and she took it across the room to her cauldron.

She stopped, looked over her shoulder, and smiled. "It's not my dinner this time," she assured him.

She added some potions from a locked cabinet, stirred it all up in the pot, and chanted something Brad couldn't understand. He thought it might be Gaelic. Then she dipped the necklace into the pot and continued her chanting.

"Here you go—one enchanted amulet," she declared and handed the necklace back to him.

"Thank you. I only have this ring to offer you as payment this time," he remarked and held out the jewelry.

"Great. I needed a new ring to bless," she told him with a smile.

When Brad left, her smile got even bigger. He had no idea what she had just done, and the ring was going to give her the perfect connection.

Chapter 59

Seth ran in every direction to locate the vampire. He was a blur to the people in the crowd, who were still watching the Golden Dragon snake its way by.

Zephryne had ducked under the dragon costume and walked along with the men and women operating it. The Lycan wouldn't be able to track her among all the humans—they would mask her scent. Speaking of scent, she was getting thirsty. She bit into the woman in front of her while locking the human between her steely arms. The woman's screams were drowned out by the shouts of the crowd and the others under the dragon costume. Zephryne held the dead woman's body up while the dragon moved along the street and around the block. Then it was time to move on, so she dropped the body to the pavement and ducked back out of the costume.

The crowd's screams turned from excitement to screams of fear as the people piled in toward the dragon, which seemed to be breaking apart. Seth stopped to look and saw the dead body. He also used his Lycan eyesight and saw the bite marks. He raced through the crowd to the other side of the street, but the scent trailed off among all the humans. It was time to give up his hunt and go back to Julia to be sure she was safe.

Chapter 60

"What are you doing here, Brad?" Julia asked in surprise.

"The question is, what are you doing here since you are supposed to be home in bed? Or maybe you'd rather be in my bed again," he suggested with a perverted smile.

The idea almost made her gag. "Um, no, and who are you—my mother?"

"No? Why the change of heart? You were all too happy to be in my bed yesterday."

"Brad, I have no idea what all happened yesterday, but I can assure you it was a mistake, and I won't be repeating it," she declared.

Just then, her cell phone rang, and she saw it was Melanie. "Long time, no see," she answered.

"Hey, girlie. Did you ever hook up with that hot guy?" her friend asked.

"Wow, right to it, eh?" She glanced at Brad, who looked bored, and mentally willed him away. "Yes, I did. Now, what's up?"

"I knew it, you lucky slut. I miss you, so when can we get together? I want to meet your fella," she exclaimed.

"I don't know," Julia answered while looking at the entrance door.

She didn't even know where her "fella" was at the moment, and she was mad as hell that he'd so rudely taken off the way he did. At least Brad had gotten up and left—Mel had good timing for once.

Just then, she saw Seth walking into the restaurant. "Mel, I have to go. I'll ask Seth and get back to you soon."

"Ooh...Seth-h-h," Melanie drew his name out. "What a sexy name. Don't take too long getting back to me. See ya." The line went dead.

"Why did you run off like that? Are you nuts? I almost went home!" she laid right into him.

He held one hand up. "I'm sorry, but it was important."

"What was so damn important that you'd bolt and leave me alone? Was that just payback for earlier?" she accused.

"No, my sweet." He really didn't know how to explain that he was chasing a vampire. *Three days.* "I sensed danger, and I wanted to make sure you were safe. Can we just drop it for now please?"

Julia stared at him with wide eyes. "What the hell are you talking about? How can you 'sense danger'? Are you friggin' Spiderman or something?" she asked, irate. She had heard some lame excuses before, but that one took the cake.

"Something like that. Would that turn you on?" he inquired, trying to lighten the mood.

"Whatever." She rolled her eyes at him. "Don't tell me the truth then. Just know that is was very rude of you to ditch me like that."

"I'm sorry, baby." He took her hand and kissed it.

The waiter showed up then and took their orders. They both decided to just eat from the buffet.

When they sat down with their plates, he took her hand again. "I'm sorry I left you all alone in here." He gave her puppy dog eyes in an attempt to still win her good graces back.

Julia didn't tell Seth about Brad showing up. She just wanted to forget that little visit.

"My friend Melanie called and kept me company over the phone. She wants to meet you, so do you feel like getting together with her for a drink tonight at Howl?"

"Yes, I'd like to meet your friends," he responded with a grin.

"Oh, there's just her."

"Just one friend? You're such a nice person, though. I figured you'd have lots of friends," he told her, hoping the flattery would continue to soften her.

"No. I have trust issues, so I don't let many people in. I've seen the damage people can inflict on you if you let them." Then she wondered to herself how it was that Seth was getting close to her. *It can't only be because of the great sex.*

"That must be what Madame Elmira was referring to when she read your past," he suggested.

She sucked in her bottom lip. "Yeah, maybe, if you believe in those readings. So, what's next for our day of fun?" She didn't want to talk about her past, and she didn't want to discuss the future that had been described for her either. She wasn't ready to get that close with him. "Will you finally show me your house?"

They were already done eating from the buffet, and she was ready to move because just sitting there would mean more conversation. Conversations she might not want to have—if he asked about work, that would make her think about Brad.

Seth knew he could stall for only so long. He pretended to pat his pockets for something. "Hey, I just realized I left my wallet at Madame Elmira's shop. Let me run and fetch it while you get dessert. I'll be right back. I promise." He gave her a quick peck on the forehead and left.

Chapter 61

Madame Elmira looked up from the book she was reading. "You're back, so what's wrong?"

"I need your help with something. I need a potion that will make Julia forget something," Seth replied.

"I'm not sure I have anything for that. What does she need to forget if I may ask Ki—" She remembered he didn't like the formality. "Seth?"

"Do you remember when I told you I had to kill one human to avoid being discovered?"

She looked down at the ground and nodded. He knew it was monstrosity in her eyes, and it would be worse for Julia.

"I think she's been to the den—I mean the house—I reside in. It belonged to that hunter, and she's dated him before. She wants to see where I live, and I can't keep holding it off. I don't want to have to kill anyone else to take over their dwelling. I just need her to forget that she's been there before."

"Oh, that's tricky. If you try to affect one memory, you'll really be affecting all memories. We can't select one thing from the mind to forget—not even with magic. Messing with her mind is going to be a big gamble. That is if I can even find something that will help. Are you sure you want to take that big of a risk?"

"Well, I'd like to avoid it, but you know what might happen if I don't have my queen by the end of the blood moon. Can we afford not to take the risk?"

She considered his question. "I suppose you're right about that, but isn't there a way to just avoid your dwelling until after the blood moon?"

"No, she has her heart set on seeing where I live, and I can tell she's growing suspicious. She might even think I have a wife and family hidden. I need to take her somewhere."

"Okay, fair enough. Let me even see what I have that might help at all. I'll be right back." Madame Elmira went behind a curtain, and Seth could hear her rummaging through cabinets and drawers. Three long minutes passed before she reappeared with a small vial of purple liquid. "I think this will do the trick for you. At least I hope so"— she looked away while blushing—"I had a little mix up while making a potion for a customer once, and this is what was created. She took it to overcome a phobia, but it ended up making her forget things. Fortunately, it made her forget her phobia too," she laughed. "Now, don't give her too much because we don't want her to forget too much— including you. Just one drop in her drink at least thirty minutes before taking her to your house should hopefully do it, okay?" She handed him the small vial.

"Okay, just one drop. Got it. Thank you for your help." He surprised her with a kiss on the cheek.

She chuckled and told him, "Remember, there is a revelation coming to you soon. The truth will be coming out about something, so be ready for it. The stars say you hold the key to the answers you seek."

"Right. The truth will be about Julia becoming my queen because there is no other way I will have it. Anyone else is just unacceptable," he stated flatly.

"I hope you're right," she whispered as he sauntered out the door.

Chapter 62

Brad went home sulking. He thought about the argument Julia had had with Seth in the restaurant. He knew the Lycan had been chasing after Zephryne. She had been following him to make sure he was trying to find the key—the queen—for Prince Armando. Brad felt a wave of embarrassment as it occurred to him that she might have seen his unsuccessful encounter with the Gypsy woman earlier. The Gypsy was going to get her comeuppance, and it was time to hunt her down.

He touched the Black Dragon amulet. "Let's go find her," he said to the charm. It would help him locate the little bitch.

Brad headed back toward the edge of Chinatown, where there was a large Gypsy community, and walked around. There was a bonfire going, and some men were practicing a juggling act while the women were setting tables with food, and children were running about. Sadly, he didn't see Ofelia anywhere. He did, however, see another young woman wandering off by herself whom he could test. He was, after all, running out of time. He looked up at the clear blue sky. *Just three days.* A wicked smile graced his lips—the world had no idea what it was in store for. He followed the young woman into a tent.

"Who are you?" the woman demanded, and she looked like she was about to scream, but he closed in on her and covered her mouth.

"Well, I'm either your salvation or the grim reaper. It hasn't been determined yet," he whispered with a sadistic smile. "I possess the power to either make you a queen or the evening news. Do you follow so far?"

The frightened woman nodded slowly with his hand still over her mouth.

"Are you wearing your pendant or the evil eye?"

She nodded again.

"Then use them to protect yourself. Show me how strong you are. Show me you are the one I'm looking for."

He was almost pleading with the woman. He had to find the key, and he didn't want it to be Julia. He began to squeeze the Gypsy's neck, but she didn't fight him off— she couldn't fight him off. She stared into his eyes, while the life was squeezed right out of her, with the same blank eyes that he cut afterward.

Brad left the tent in search of Ofelia. It had to be her. It just had to be her.

Chapter 63

Seth sat back down at their table in the restaurant. "I found it," he told her and held up his wallet for emphasis. "Now, where were we?"

"You were avoiding taking me to your house. Are you that ashamed of where you live, because you shouldn't be." She tapped her fingers restlessly on the table.

"No, we can go there if you want to. But, first, would you like some more tea? I'm going to have another glass."

"Maybe I could drink a little more." She looked around for their server.

"Okay, I'll go get it while I pay the check," he offered. He got up and took the glasses with him. The cashier refilled the glasses for him, and he put a drop from the vial into hers and stirred it with her straw before returning to the table. He hoped it didn't have a taste. "Here you go." He put the drink in front of her and sat back down. Then he raised his own glass and clinked hers. "Cheers," he said.

"Okay, cheers," she replied and took a big sip. She started to cough, and he thought he was busted. "Ugh," she groaned with a sour face. "They made a bad batch that time." She pushed the glass away from herself. "Are you done stalling? I'm ready to see your mysterious bachelor's pad."

"Yes, let's go," he replied, hoping with all his heart that she drank enough of the potion for it to work and that it would work in time. Everything depended on having her trust.

Chapter 64

Seth was worried that the taxi ride wouldn't be long enough for the potion to work, so he needed to stall. "Driver, go through the park and drive around the lake first." He turned to Julia and commented, "It's such a pretty day, let's drag it out a bit."

The driver interrupted, "Did you see the guy jump over the Golden Dragon? That was insane man! I didn't get to see it, but my cousin did, and he told me all about it."

"What? What on earth are you talking abo—" Julia's hand flew to her forehead, and she closed her eyes. "Whoa!"

"What's wrong, Julia?" Seth demanded. "Are you all right, sweetie?"

"I-I-I'm okay. I just got a little dizzy for a second, but it's gone. Now say that again about the Golden Dragon." She looked up front at the cabbie.

"A man jumped right over it! It must have been part of the show or something crazy like that," he told her animatedly.

"That's impossible. The Golden Dragon must be at least seven feet tall," she said while fanning herself. "Can you turn on the AC? It's hot in here."

Seth felt ashamed. He hoped she wasn't going to have a bunch of side effects from the potion.

Before the driver could say any more about the preposterous story, Julia's cell phone rang. It was Melanie again. Julia mumbled to herself, "She never did have any patience." She unlocked the phone and answered, "I knew you wouldn't wait for me to call you."

"I knew you'd take all day about it. What did lover boy say?" she asked.

Julia looked at her watch, but the numbers were fuzzy. She squinted her eyes and could finally make out that it was 3:00. "We can meet you at 7:00 at Howl. Don't be late."

"I won't be," Melanie assured her before hanging up. Julia would bet otherwise, however. Melanie had the belief that nothing really began until she got there.

She looked out the car window at the crystal waters of a small lake. "Where are we?" she asked Seth.

"We are by Golden Gate Park. Remember? We were going for a drive," he answered while studying her face for a reaction, for an indication that the potion was kicking in.

"Oh, yeah, I remember. You came up with another way to stall taking me to your house. Waiting for the wife and kids to leave?" she teased.

Uh oh. Maybe it's not working yet. Maybe it's not going to. "Ha-ha. That's funny, and no, they left hours ago." He winked at her, and she playfully slapped his arm. "We should be at the house in about ten minutes." Hopefully, that would be enough time for the potion to kick in.

Soon, the cab pulled up to the house, and Seth paid the driver. Once again, he was grateful that the hunter had a lot of cash laying around his house. He supposed the man must not have trusted banks. He studied Julia's face as she got out of the car and looked for any signs of recognition. She was squinting from the sun, though, so it was difficult to tell. His stomach turned as he waited for her to say something, and he tried to think of an explanation in case she did.

They stepped into the foyer, and her eyes started blinking rapidly as she looked around the area and adjoining living room.

Oh no. She remembers.

"This is a nice house, but I'm having the weirdest sense of déjà vu." She stepped back outside into the front yard and looked harder at the house. Then she went back inside and started walking around and studying everything. "I feel like I've been here before, but that doesn't make much sense. Oh well," she commented and shrugged. "How about a tour?"

Whew, that was close. "Sure thing, ma'am." He bowed to her and then gestured down the expansive hallway. He took her on the complete tour of his den, saving the bedroom for last. He was glad that he had hidden the photos, trophies, and everything else with the hunter's name or face on it.

When they got to the bedroom, Julia sniffed the air and looked at him. "Do you have a dog? I can smell dog."

He had to think fast—he knew that she was smelling his Lycan form. He sometimes shifted in his sleep. "No, but maybe the previous owner did. I moved in recently and I haven't had time to shampoo the carpets yet."

"Oh, okay." She seemed satisfied at first, but then she started looking around the room. "I've been in a bedroom before with walls painted this color. It's called eggplant, I think. It's not a common color choice." Her eyes squinted at every detail as she walked around the spacious master bedroom. Then she put her hands to her temples and rubbed. "This is giving me a migraine. I know I've been in this house before, but I just can't remember. Oh, it's so frustrating!"

"Here, sweetie. Sit down, and I'll rub your temples, neck, and shoulders for you." He pointed to the bed.

She did as he suggested and let her body soften under the wondrous touch of his firm hands. She could feel herself melt as he worked her muscles over until the tension left her neck and shoulders.

Seth needed to distract her. He leaned in and planted soft kisses on her neck. She didn't protest, so he let his hands roam over her body and up to her breasts where he ever so gently squeezed. He felt her buds grow rigid under his palms, and he rubbed slow circles over them, which made her gasp. He watched her face go soft as she relaxed, and then her lips parted slightly while he pinched her protruding tips. Her eyes remained closed the entire time, and her breathing was ragged. He turned her chin toward himself and claimed her lips in a kiss that sent tingles along every nerve in her body. His arms wrapped around her waist, and he lay her down on the bed. She clutched his biceps while his hand went up under her shirt and pushed its way under her bra to meet her scalding flesh.

"Oh," escaped her lips.

He was tormenting her, and she felt an ache for him rise from her middle and spread throughout her body. Flames licked her pleasure points as they ached to be touched by him. She ran her hands up under his shirt and caressed the corded muscle defining his chest and back. He had such a powerful brawny frame. He was very masculine, and the proof of it was pressing hard against her. It was begging to be free from its cotton barriers, and she wanted to help it along. She reached down and tugged at the button on his shorts.

"Here, let me help you," he said in a deep, husky voice thick with lust. He pushed her hand aside and unfastened the shorts, and his hot distended flesh sprung forth.

Julia wrapped her grip around his fullness and stroked him. She urgently needed him pulsating inside her writhing body.

Seth matched her desires with his own, and it took him only a minute to have them both naked. Her skin seared his as they pressed against one another. He used one hand to gently part her milky-white thighs and then ran his fingertips lightly up them to her molten center.

"Oh, God," Julia cried out as he tormented her intimate parts with talented fingers.

They slipped within her and brought forth convulsions of ecstasy. His mouth matched the rhythm of his hand and worked its way over her breasts. He tugged on her pink crests with his teeth before drawing them into his wet mouth. She moved her hands through his hair and gently pulled. Then she needed to touch every inch of him, so she ran them over his magnificent hard body as far as she could reach. When he rose over her, she grabbed onto his perfectly formed, cast-iron buttocks and squeezed while he penetrated her moist softness.

They moaned in unison as he embedded the hard pulse of his arousal inside her fiery depths. He rocked her body in slow, measured strokes, and the room was filled with moans and gasps of pleasure.

Julia felt her body being engulfed with wave after wave of all-consuming rapture. She fell into such an abyss of ecstasy, that she didn't know if she would climb back out of it. She didn't know if she ever wanted to.

Seth wrapped his strong arms around her and rolled her over on top of himself. Julia slowly slid her body down his hardened staff and took over the lovemaking. She arched her back and glided her hips back and forth in a fevered pitch of pure desire.

It didn't take long before stars filled both their eyes while explosions of unrivaled bliss wracked their bodies. Ragged gasps filled the air as she rolled off him and nestled herself against his side. Feeling overwhelmed by pleasure and something else too—something like a tug on her heart—Julia closed her eyes and drifted off into a deep and restful sleep.

Chapter 65

Brad looked all over the Gypsy camp for Ofelia, and after about an hour of searching, not including the time it took to test and dispatch the other Gypsy, he finally saw her. She was outside a tent talking to another woman. He decided to wait until she was alone.

Screaming suddenly came from the tent he'd already visited. "Genoveva! No!"

He watched as the camp rushed to see what the screaming was about, and when Ofelia ran by with the crowd, he grabbed her and yanked her into an empty tent. Before her own screams could pierce the air, Brad hit her hard enough on the back of the head to render her unconscious. Then he carried her to his car and drove home. Nobody even looked up to notice them

Chapter 66

After what felt like hours, Julia woke up in Seth's arms. She looked at her watch while he traced his fingertips lightly over her body. It had only been about twenty minutes.

"I fell asleep," she mumbled groggily.

"Yes, I know. You snored a little," he laughed.

"Oh, that's just wonderful. My head is so fuzzy. Did I have alcohol today?" she questioned and rubbed her temples.

"No, you had tea with lunch. I hope you aren't coming down with something," he told her and gave her a squeeze. He hoped the potion wasn't making her sick.

"Yeah, me too," she agreed. "Where are we?" She looked around the room with a dazed look on her face.

"We're at my house, remember?" He was glad the potion hadn't worn off yet, but he felt somewhat guilty.

"Maybe…I'm not sure. I'm still sleepy," she mumbled with a big yawn.

"I can see that. Are you too sleepy to go out tonight for drinks with your friend? If you'd rather not go, that's all right with me. I wouldn't mind keeping you all to myself." He kissed her forehead.

"My friend? Oh, yeah, drinks with Melanie. What time is that again?" She looked up at him with glassy eyes.

"You told her 7:00. Are you still okay with that?"

"Yes, that's fine with me. I should feel okay by then. I feel like I'm forgetting something else, though. Was there anything else we had to do today? What *did* we do today? I can't remember much." She grimaced and wrung her hands.

"Well, we saw Madame Elmira, and she told us that our futures were going to be filled with love, and then we saw the Golden Dragon parade. Are you sure you feel up to going out?" He wondered how long the potion was supposed to last. He worried it might affect her job, and even worse, he worried it might affect them. He wished he knew what to expect.

"Yeah, I'll be okay," she assured him. "I guess we need to go check on Oscar then. I need to walk him and check his food and water before we go out tonight."

Good. Remembering Oscar is a great sign. "Of course, we definitely have to tend to him first. We can go now if you like," he offered.

She looked at him thoughtfully—she was feeling horny. "Well, maybe in a couple of minutes. I need reminding of why we are naked first." She reached her hand under the covers and grazed her fingers over his taut thigh and then over his thickening length.

"Oh, you're a little vixen, aren't you? I'd be happy to remind you why we're both naked." He swept her into his arms and made passionate love to her again.

Chapter 67

After they made love, Seth felt it was best to leave the house quickly, just in case her memory started coming back. She kept glancing around the house curiously, even as they made their exit.

"I just can't shake the feeling of familiarity," she told him.

"It happens to everyone. It will come to you eventually," he replied but hoped not. "Let's go see Ossy. He probably needs to go out, right?"

"Yes, I'm sure he does. Are you going to drive?"

Good question. He'd studied and practiced driving using the hunter's car in empty lots and low traffic areas. He was still amazed by all the things and conveniences modern-day humans had.

He decided that to boost his confidence and aid him, he needed to wear his pendant of λύκος. He hadn't been wearing it around Julia in order to avoid any questions she might have regarding it. Also, he risked its recognition in public by Gypsies, and that could cause some unwelcomed attention. He didn't need the world to know that the king of the Lycans had mysteriously woken up. However, as the blood moon drew closer, he needed to wear it always. It would come in handy with the vampires around.

"Sure, I can drive if you want. Let me go get the right keys," he told her before going back into the house and grabbing the pendant, which he hid under his shirt.

On the way to her house, Julia teased him about his driving skills. "You drive like an old lady," she laughed.

"I have to be careful because I have precious cargo," he replied with a wink.

Fortunately, it was a short drive to her place. He opened her door for her while sniffing the air for any signs of vampires in the vicinity, and he was relieved when he didn't smell any. He wondered how many were roaming the earth in the current year. The Lycan clans, in his time, had done well to keep their numbers low, but since his clan's defeat, he could only imagine that their numbers had grown. Hopefully, few were residing in the United States. They, too, had originated in Romania and the outlying areas and then traveled abroad when man settled the new world. The Lycans had followed them.

The vampire smell that had been in Julia's hallway earlier was, thankfully, no longer noticeable. She opened her apartment door, and Oscar was indeed happy to see them. After jumping up to greet Julia, he laid down on his back in front of Seth, just as he had done so every time before.

"Why do you think he does that?" She shook her head at the dog and then looked up at Seth. "He never does that with anyone else."

Seth smiled at Oscar. "He recognizes me as the alpha. He's showing submissiveness when he does that." There was truth in his words. The dog knew who was boss in their canine to canine relationship.

"Alpha, huh? That's kind of sexy," Julia said while wrapping her arms around his waist.

He laughed at her. "You sure are feeling randy today—not that I'm complaining."

"Yeah, I am. I think maybe it's the full moon coming. It's a blood moon too, you know?"

"I do know," he answered while gazing out the kitchen window at the sky. Then he noticed the flowers by the sink. "Who's my competition?"

She blinked her eyes at him, "Your what?"

He looked at her with a grave expression. "Who are the flowers from?"

"Oh! I forgot about those. Honestly, I don't know who they're from. They were left outside my door, and there was no card with them."

"Does that happen to you a lot?" he asked while walking over to the blood orchids. "Do admirers just leave you gifts outside your door?"

She looked at him and studied his features for any sign of humor, but his face was serious. "You sound like you're jealous, and no, I don't usually receive random gifts."

"Jealous? No, just protective of what is mine," he stated while checking the flowers out.

Among the floral scent was another—vampire. *A damned vampire left the flowers! Probably just to let me know how close they'd gotten.* What other reason could there be? Seth's first instinct was to throw the vase across the room to shatter it into a thousand pieces, but he had to control his temper. Julia wouldn't understand, and he wasn't ready to tell her. But very soon he would be; he had no choice in the matter. *Maybe tonight.*

"I'll throw them out if it bothers you," she offered. She was standing next to him and had placed her hand on his arm. "I only kept them because they smell nice."

"No, you don't have to do that. I can handle the competition"—he looked down and smiled—"You're a beautiful woman, and I need to get used to other men wanting you for themselves." He wrapped his arms around her and gave her tight squeeze. "However, no one else can have you because you're mine, Julia Stevens." He left no room for argument in his tone.

She looked at him wide-eyed. Normally there was no way in hell she'd let a man be possessive of her like that, but for some reason, she kind of liked that Seth was. Still, she considered slowing things down with him. She didn't want to see anyone else, but she didn't want to be claimed either. *Do I?* She glanced at her watch. She had to get a move on, or Melanie would gripe about her being late for once.

"I'm just going to go change my clothes and touch up my makeup," she mentioned before leaving him in the living room. "You boys play nice."

Julia chose a blood-red dress that was low-cut in the front and red spiked heels, so she wouldn't feel like a Pygmy next to Seth. He wolf-whistled when she returned to the living room.

"Wow, look at you! Isn't she gorgeous, Ossy?" He looked at the dog, who had been napping at his feet. Oscar yawned and rolled onto his side.

Julia laughed, "He's seen me in this before."

Seth took her hand and twirled her. "Well, I could just eat you up," he growled sensuously.

"Thanks, but later," she purred and winked. "I don't want to be late. I actually want to be able to bust her for being late, *yet again*." She rolled her eyes, but then she smiled mischievously. "I'll drive, so we can get there on time."

Seth laughed with her and then sniffed for vampire scent in the hallway and outside the building. Everything was all clear, but for how long?

Chapter 68

Ofelia woke up and noticed two things: her head was pounding, and she was bound and gagged. Having no idea what had happened, she looked at her surroundings. It was dimly lit, though, so she couldn't make much out, but she assumed it was a basement. Unexpectedly, she heard laughter from somewhere nearby, and her body jerked in response.

"It's about time you woke up, *Ofelia*," a man's voice snarled.

Since he knew her name, the attack, obviously, hadn't been random. Her heart rate increased, and she wriggled in an attempt to loosen her bonds while a cold sweat dripped into her eyes.

"What you did to me today wasn't very nice. Nope, it wasn't very nice at all," her abductor tormented her in an evil tone.

Ofelia tried to respond to him; she wanted to ask her kidnapper what the abduction was all about, but only muffled cries came through the duct tape that was covering her mouth. She tried to focus, first on his voice, which sounded familiar, and then on the events of the day. She remembered him then—he was the man from the alley; he was the man she'd cut. *But how did he find me and get me here, wherever here is? And, more importantly, how can I escape?*

She heard footsteps heading toward her, and she tried with all her might to concentrate on the amulets she wore. Was she even still wearing them? She couldn't be sure. Then she got her answer.

"Looking for these?" the man asked her, and she heard clinking of metal against metal—he'd taken her amulets. "They weren't helping that much anyway, obviously," her captor laughed. "I mean, really, what were you going to do to me? They didn't stop me before; that was just trickery on your part, but it won't happen again. In fact, maybe I should give you a taste of your own medicine. Maybe I should kick you in your crotch and slice into you with that knife. What do you think?"

He'd stopped talking, so Ofelia assumed he was waiting for an answer. She shook her head vigorously side to side.

"No, of course not"—he descended upon her— "You wouldn't want to damage that pretty figure of yours with a horrible scar. The prince wouldn't like that either." She cocked her head in confusion, so he went on to explain, "Are you wondering who the prince is? Well, he might just be the man of your dreams, or maybe it's your nightmares, but aren't all marriages like that really?" Confusion still clouded her eyes, but tears did too. "Now, now," he pretended to coddle her. "Every bride has jitters before the big day. It will all be okay. As long as you are the one, that is. You're a strong Gypsy, but you haven't shown me yet your full strength. I have to know that you're the one meant for the prince, or we'll both be dead."

He walked up to her and put her talisman and evil eye back on her. He felt a little sting from touching them, but he wanted to feel their full force. She had to turn on her power and prove to him that he hadn't made a grave error.

He ripped the tape off her mouth, cut the bindings on her hands, and told her, "Show me what you can do. Give it your best shot."

Chapter 69

Seth and Julia arrived at Howl at 7:00 sharp, and much to Julia's surprise, Melanie was there already. She waved the couple over to her table.

"Ha! I beat you for a change, and I bet you thought I'd be late." She was talking to Julia, but her eyes were fixated on Seth as she looked him up and down repeatedly.

"Put your tongue back in your mouth," Julia chastised her. "Melanie, this is Seth. Seth, the woman staring at you shamelessly is Melanie."

"How are you?" Seth asked and shook her hand. He knew she was staring, and he thought it was rude of her to do that to her friend.

"So, Mel, where is your latest love? Will he be joining us tonight?" Julia wondered.

Melanie looked at Julia like she was crazy. "Love? It was hardly love; it was just sex, and that's over. It turned out the prick is married. Can you believe it? I mean the nerve of some men." She looked at Seth with a steady glare. "You're not married, are you?"

"Melanie!" Julia screeched at her.

Indeed, she could believe it where her naive friend was concerned. She loved Melanie dearly, but the woman had terrible judgment when it came to men. She looked for love in all the wrong places and in all the wrong ways.

"Okay, okay. I'm sorry for assuming the worst. Anyway, how about you two? Is it love or just lust?" She winked at Seth.

Julia coughed and shot her friend a dirty look. "We are doing just fine, thank you. We are getting to know each other."

Seth felt downhearted like a cub whose favorite toy just broke. Sure, they hadn't said the words yet, but he was in love, and he was going to tell her later when they were alone.

"Well, don't forget that Madame Elmira saw love in both our futures," he reminded Julia with a grin.

She blushed. "I think I need a drink. Where's our server?" She looked around the room, avoiding eye contact with both Melanie and Seth.

"Madame Elmira?" Melanie wasn't letting it slide by. "Did you go see a Gypsy, Julia? I'm shocked." She placed a hand over her heart for emphasis.

"Yes, but it was just for fun. I'm not sure that I believe in what she said, but it was entertaining," Julia replied with a casual shrug.

"Well, I believed her, but then again, I want to, and that makes a difference. Now, what would you like to drink? I'll go get it," Seth offered.

"I'll have a piña colada, please," she said softly.

She could tell she'd hurt his feelings, and she felt bad about it. She needed to explain to him that she wasn't looking for a committed relationship, at least not yet. She knew she needed to tell him later when they were alone.

Seth went to the bar to get Julia's drink and decided to try one himself, so he ordered two piña coladas from the same bartender that had been flirting with her the other night. The brash bartender checked her out again while setting the drinks down in front of Seth. He'd tried to be casual about it, but the Lycan was no idiot. He gave the man a low, threatening growl, which made him back away.

"Whoa…settle down big guy. I was just looking, dude," the man defended himself.

"Well, I suggest you admire someone else because she is off limits to you." He could have taken it further, but he didn't want to cause a scene in front of his queen. It wasn't the time nor the place. Also, if he lost his temper, he'd likely kill the man, and he didn't want to do that. He wanted to kill vampires.

Back at their table, he tried the drink and must have made a sour face because both women started laughing at him.

"Have you ever had a piña colada before?" Julia chuckled.

"No, I sure haven't. Actually, I'm not much of a drinker at all." He took another sip. "It's not too bad, though."

Melanie held her glass up for a toast. "To old friends and new ones." Presumably, she was addressing both Seth and Julia, but she only kept her eyes on him.

Julia started to feel a little bit jealous. She wasn't sure how she felt about Seth yet, but she did know that she didn't like the idea of sharing him.

She addressed Melanie, "So, now that you aren't dating your Latin lover anymore, are you looking again? I see a couple of guys checking you out, and there's always the cute bartender." Seth shifted in his chair when she said the last part, so she instantly regretted it. She wasn't trying to make him jealous, so she added, "Of course, none of them are as handsome as Seth."

"No, they are certainly not," her friend agreed.

Melanie couldn't take her eyes off Julia's boyfriend. He was so brawny, and she wanted him. It figured that Julia had seen him first—she always got the best-looking guys. It wasn't that Melanie wasn't pretty, because she was. She was petite with long black hair, sparkling green eyes, and nice curves. She never had a problem with getting men, but they were never the caliber that Julia attracted. Julia didn't even want a man around, whereas she did. She hated to be alone.

Well, if her friend threw him away too, she'd be the first in line to console him. In fact, while Julia was a dear friend, she was ready to snatch him up right then—*all is fair in love and war, right?*

Chapter 70

Tressa sat in her chair and petted her boa constrictor. She looked at the ring she was wearing and smiled. It was the ring the dark Gypsy had given her as his payment for her service. It had a special purpose for her, and it was time to use it.

She wrapped the boa around her shoulders and walked over to the cauldron and her cabinets full of potions and ingredients. She opened the biggest book of spells she had and flipped to the end. There it was—a special spell that would open a window through either a mirror or a ring. She put the ring into her cauldron and, one by one, added the necessary ingredients. She added: caraway, bay leaves, praying mantis legs, atropa belladonna, glechoma hederacea, and goat's blood. She stirred the concoction and chanted the magic words.

It was time to test it, so she used a set of tongs to remove the ring from the kettle, and even though it was hot, she slipped it on. She closed her eyes and concentrated. Her mind's eye could see what the dark Gypsy was up to. He was going to wake the vampire prince, Prince Armando, and present him with a queen. Then the army of the undead would rise and battle the Lycans for dominance over the world. This interested her—she'd like to be the vampire queen. What a great source of power that would be when added to her own. It was power she'd long waited for and deserved. It was power she'd been deprived of back when she was just a Gypsy, and she was going to go after it. For the first time in ten years, she left her cottage on the bluffs and went looking for the

dark Gypsy and the woman he was holding captive.
She had her own plans for the young Gypsy woman.

Chapter 71

A band began playing, and Julia, after her third drink, was ready to dance. She and Melanie started off dancing while Seth just watched. Melanie was doing everything she could to get his attention, including making an ass of herself because he wasn't responding. The more he ignored her, the harder she tried.

Seth had experienced this before, back when a Gypsy was desperate to become his queen. His hands clenched the table hard as he remembered the woman. Her name was Isis Rosci, and brokenhearted from his rejection, she had turned her love for him into hatred. She began practicing witchcraft and helped the vampire king curse him. Seth was so angered by the memory that he felt his body tremble, and the table cracked from the pressure of his grip. His body was trying to shift, and he was fighting it with all his might.

Carefully, he approached Julia on the dance floor and simply told her that he needed some fresh air and would be back in a few minutes. She offered to go with him, but he told her that he didn't want her to see him get sick.

Once he was outside, he went to the woods, undressed, and shifted. He tore through the trees while all the emotions he'd felt over the past few days—the good and bad—poured out of him. He howled at the sky and at the moon, which would be full all too soon. He needed more time with Julia—he needed more time to win her love. Another howl erupted from him, and it was louder than before. It shook the forest, and animals scattered everywhere. Seth lunged at a bear that was chasing down an elk, and he tore into it like he was starved. That wasn't enough, though, so he found a mountain lion and ate that too. It wasn't even because he was hungry; he just needed to release his frustration.

Once he calmed down and cleaned the blood off himself in a creek, he went back to Julia. She and Melanie were still dancing, but they weren't alone. Two men were dancing with them, and one had the audacity to be rubbing up against his queen. Seth approached the man, put a hand on his shoulder, and yanked him away from her so hard that the man went sailing across the room into the wall. The other man backed away from the women immediately, and the whole club, including Julia, stared at him like he was a monster. Seth felt the tremors again and knew that he needed to get out of there, but he wasn't leaving without his queen.

He looked at Melanie and pointed an accusing finger. "You are a terrible friend to Julia," he growled at her.

"What is that?" Julia interrupted by pointing to his shirt.

The pendant of λύκος was glowing underneath his shirt. He didn't know what it meant, but they needed to go—immediately. Julia was stumbling from the alcohol, so he just picked her up and carried her like a child.

"We need to leave now." His tone was serious, but she started laughing.

He would just have to let her sleep the alcohol off and tell her that he loved her in the morning. He took her car keys from her purse and drove back to her apartment building.

After putting her to bed, he took Oscar out for his walk. They both sniffed the air and gave it the all clear of vampire stench before heading back inside.

Seth checked on Julia one more time, and she was already sound asleep. Oscar looked up at her and whined.

"Don't worry, Ossy. She'll sleep it off." Seth spent the night, but he slept on the couch close to the front door. Oscar did too.

Chapter 72

Julia woke up and looked out her bedroom window. The first quarter moon shone brightly, but everything in her room was cast in shadows and spinning. She'd had too much to drink. She didn't even know how she'd made it home. Suddenly, she saw something move past her window, and she screamed.

Seth sprang from the couch and ran into Julia's bedroom. "What's wrong?" He rushed to her side and held her.

She jumped from the sight of him at first, but then, trembling in his arms, she pointed an unsteady finger at the window and told him, "I saw something move out there."

"Oh, sweetheart, it's okay. It was probably just a bird or a squirrel," he soothed her with his voice while rocking her gently. "But let me check to show you that everything is okay."

He opened the locked window, and it hit him like a wet blanket—the stink of vampire. Seth jumped out the window, shifted mid-air, and hit the ground running. He left his shredded clothes in a pile and a terrified and confused Julia back up in her room, staring at the window.

"What did I just see?" she wondered aloud. "That couldn't have just happened," she whispered right before her stomach lunged forward and sent her to the bathroom. After she vomited, she passed out on the bathmat while Oscar lay next to her, growling protectively.

Chapter 73

Seth ran rampant around the building and into the woods—he was on the vampire's trail. He didn't know if any humans had seen him, and he didn't care. This vampire wasn't going to be a threat any longer. As he powered through the trees, he noticed a pack of wolves running alongside him, trying to keep up. *Brother would fight with brother.* Even though the Lycan stood seven-feet-tall and on two legs, like a man, the wolves knew he was canis lupus. Seth howled, and the pack answered. Then the pendant he still wore began to glow, and he knew he was closing in on his enemy.

It took only two hundred more yards to find the cowardice vampire hiding inside a barn. The female vampire was crouched down behind a barrel, and she lunged at Seth. He used one clawed hand to backhand her and send her flying across the barn. She quickly recovered and leapt though the air at him again, trying to bite into his shoulder, but he deflected the wound and chomped into her neck. Blood spurted forth like a fountain as she struggled to get free. His grip, though, was too strong, and he used one more bite to finish severing her head. The body and the head both crumpled to the ground.

Just as he was going to pick the body up in order to dispose of it in the woods, he heard shouting and a shotgun blast. The owner was on his way to the barn. Seth left the body and ran out the back door and into the woods with the pack of wolves close on his heels. He ran all the way to his den and broke in to get clothes. Then he ran, as a human, back to Julia's apartment building. The wolf pack still followed even though he was in human form again.

Seth climbed up the trellis outside Julia's window and climbed back into her bedroom, hoping he hadn't been seen by anyone. He found Julia asleep on the bathroom floor with the dog next to her. He picked both of them up and carried them to the bed. He lay Oscar at the foot of the bed and then climbed in with Julia cradled in his arms. He fell asleep with her just as the sun was coming up over the horizon. *Two days. Just two days.*

Chapter 74

April 13, 2014

Tressa found the dark Gypsy's lair just as the sun was coming up. She peeked into the basement windows because that's where her vision had shown her the Gypsy woman was being held captive. She could see the woman pacing her confinements and looking for a way out. At first, she didn't see the dark Gypsy, but then she saw him coming down the stairs. She sat down in the grass to watch and listen. Brad's house was in the woods, so she didn't have to worry about someone catching her spying, unless, of course, either of the Gypsies looked up and saw her peeking in. But then what could they do to her? The man couldn't do much after what she'd done to his amulet. She doubted he even knew about that yet, but by the looks of things, he would find out soon enough.

As he approached the Gypsy woman, she braced herself for a fight. She held her amulets up and muttered a threat in Romani, which Tressa hadn't spoken in over ten years—when she turned to witchcraft and denounced her heritage—so she was rusty. She thought something was said about cutting out his tongue and spitting on his grave. *Nice.* She wasn't sure about the rest, though. The dark Gypsy just laughed at the woman; however, Tressa recognized pain on his face. Something had happened indeed.

Brad clutched his Black Dragon amulet and chanted a curse, but it didn't even phase the woman. She kept coming at him, inflicting pain with the evil eye. He had no idea what was going on, but he had to get out of there and figure it out, so he ran back up the stairs. He was even more convinced that Ofelia was the one he had been searching for, and that was terrific news for him. He had only two days left before Prince Armando would wake from his slumber.

He rubbed his hands together with an evil grin. Two days before the prophecy would be set into motion, and he would be a part of it all. *The world had no idea what was coming…*

Chapter 75

Julia woke up in Seth's arms with a pounding headache. Flashbacks of the past night went through her mind as she watched Seth sleep. She remembered drinking and dancing, and then she remembered something weird—she thought she could recall Seth jumping out her bedroom window. No, that was ridiculous—she was three stories up. She must have dreamed that.

Seth felt Julia stir and turned to face her. "How are you feeling, sweetheart? You must have gotten sick because I found you in the bathroom on the floor in the middle of the night."

Julia bolted upright in the bed, and her pounding head screamed at her. That was part of the dream—she'd seen him jump out the window and then got sick. Or did she dream it and then get sick? Yes, that made sense. She chastised herself—why would he want to jump out her window even if he could? *Because I saw something out there.* She looked at him and was about to bring it up, but she swallowed the words. He'd think she was crazy.

"My head is killing me, and I think I had a bad dream before I got sick. I don't know," she mumbled and shrugged.

Seth felt relieved that she blamed a dream for what she had seen. "Do you have any aspirin? Would that help you?" He rubbed her arm to soothe her.

"Yes, in the bathroom cabinet over the sink," she answered while rubbing her scalp.

Seth got out of bed and got her some aspirin and water to wash it down. Then he showed up with the leash and took Oscar out for his walk.

Julia smiled at his thoughtfulness, even though it hurt her face. *Ugh. Never again,* she silently promised herself. Unfortunately, it wasn't the first time she'd thought that, so she still hadn't learned her lesson.

Seth came back with Oscar right on his heels. "I started a pot of coffee for you. Would you like some breakfast? I can make a pretty mean omelet," he offered.

Her stomach clenched at the thought of food. "I'll gladly drink some coffee, but I have zero interest in eating," she grumbled.

She rolled to her side and felt him climb in behind her. He pulled her against his strong chest and wrapped his arm snugly around her. It felt wonderful and reassuring to be snuggled against him.

She reached for the TV remote and turned it on to the morning news. There was a breaking story coming from the area about seven miles west of her apartment. A woman's decapitated body had been discovered in a dairy farmer's barn during the wee hours of the morning. Apparently, the farmer had heard some growling and banging sounds and went out to investigate, and that is when he found the female. He claimed to see a pack of wolves running off into the woods nearby, but that was all he had seen. While there appeared to be animal bites at the throat, possibly causing the head to sever, animal mauling hadn't been officially ruled as the cause of death yet. The reporter claimed that animal experts would be consulted, and a local DVM would be measuring the bite radius to see if it matched up to the size of gray wolves.

Julia shuddered and clicked off the TV. "I wonder if it was a bear like in the death of my friend. But in a barn?

Would that even make sense?" She looked over her shoulder at Seth.

He shrugged with a sigh. "Perhaps, if it was looking for food, but I'm not sure. I don't know that much about bears. Are you sure you aren't hungry?"

"Yes, I'm sure, but thank you for offering."

"I think the coffee is done, so I'll go get it for you." He climbed out of bed, and she shivered from the sudden lack of his body heat.

She stopped him before he left her room. "Seth, thanks for being a good boy—" She hesitated and swallowed. "Boyfriend."

He smiled broadly. "Anything for you," he murmured with a wink while his heart did flip-flops for the first time in his entire existence.

Chapter 76

Zephryne knew something was wrong; her sister, Sasha, hadn't returned from the human's home yet. Zephryne had warned her not to go, but Sasha was young—well, she was about fifty years younger than her—and impetuous, and she'd refused to listen.

Zephryne ran through the woods, looking for her. She followed her scent trail to outside the human's dwelling, where she smelled something else too—Lycan—and it was fairly fresh. That didn't bode well. She followed the pheromones through the forest and all the way to a barn, where she picked up the strong, metallic scent of blood—her sister's blood. She watched a crowd of humans entering and exiting the barn, as she was overcome with sadness and rage. She knew just whom to take it out on too. She would confront the dark Gypsy; he was the one who had convinced Sasha to go after the mortal. He'd said that she was the key to Prince Armando's reign and that she needed to be brought to him, so he could prepare her for her nuptials.

Zephryne raced like wildfire to the Gypsy's lair nestled in the woods. She knew she couldn't kill him, no matter how desperately she wanted to, because it would take his craft to wake the dark prince. She could inflict pain on him, however, and she would.

Chapter 77

Seth felt happier than ever when he walked into the kitchen. Julia had called him her boyfriend, and that meant love was next. He just needed to win her heart. If only there was a way magic could help the process, but he knew there wasn't. Magic couldn't intervene with the emotion. Not even dark magic could facilitate love, as Isis had found out. Seth started to feel his blood simmer, so he took a deep breath—he couldn't go there again. Then he saw the flowers by the sink and thought about the vampire he'd tracked and killed. His anger, that time, was at least squelched by the satisfaction that he had killed another vampire. But then that feeling was replaced by worry. He hadn't been able to dispose of the body. What would the mortals think when they found out that the thing wasn't human? What would they say when they found the body totally decomposed to ash before they could study it? Hopefully they'd just think it had been stolen, but he would know otherwise.

"Hey! Where's my coffee?" Julia's shout came from the bedroom followed by, "Ow!"

He guessed her poor head must still be pounding. He thought about how much she must have had to drink at Howl while he'd run off into the woods to throw his tantrum. In addition to acting like a trollop, Melanie was probably a bad influence on her when it came to alcohol.

He felt himself growing angry again and took another deep breath. Then, as he made his way to the bedroom with her cup of coffee, he thought about how the pendant had glowed at the club. He still wasn't sure why because he hadn't asked anything of it. It had only ever glowed before in response to his demands. Maybe it had been his desire to tear the head off the man he'd caught flirting with Julia. That was yet another reason he should have been there. He should have been dancing with her and keeping her safe from predators.

She was sitting up in the bed and flipping through the cable channels when he entered the room. She looked up at him with a playful look of impatience.

"Well, it's about time. I ordered this hours ago," she teased.

"Oh, so we are making jokes now. Someone must be feeling better," he observed with a grin.

"Yes, the aspirin kicked in. Thanks." She took the coffee from him. "I'll be sure to tip my waiter," she joked. She continued to flip through the channels and stopped on the National Geographic channel. It was showing pictures of wolves, and that reminded her of something. "Did you hear any howling when we were at the club last night?" she asked.

"No, not that I can recall. But then again, the band was pretty loud," he replied, trying to keep his tone casual.

"I know"—she raised her brows—"That's why it's so strange, and I'm sure I wasn't the only one who heard it because people were looking out the front door when it happened to see where it was coming from."

Seth pointed at the television. "Well, they mentioned on the news that there was a pack of wolves on that man's farmland, so maybe that's what it was."

She thought about it. "Maybe, but that loud? Loud enough to be heard over a band?"

"I don't know. Maybe they came up to the building to see your gorgeous face and were wolf-whistling at you," he teased.

"Hmmm...Now who's making wise cracks?" she smirked.

"I'm serious. Did it sound anything like this?" He whistled.

Julia laughed, "No, not even close. It was scary and creepy, but it also sounded sad."

"Well, don't you worry about it, pretty woman. I'll protect you from the big bad wolf." He gave her a devilish grin and started kissing her neck. "But who will protect you from me?"

Just as she was getting into it, her cell phone interrupted. It was Melanie calling. "Good morning, and how are we feeling this morning?" Julia asked her.

"Like an ass," Melanie answered in a small voice. "I think I was a jerk around your boyfriend. Please tell him I am so, so, so sorry for acting like a slut. I was just brokenhearted that Juan turned out to be married, and I was looking for a distraction. So, I'm sorry to you, too, that I tried using yours." She wasn't sorry, but she had to lay the groundwork to be around him again. Next time she'd play it differently. Perhaps she'd be the damsel in distress since he didn't care for the seductress.

"It's Melanie, and she says to tell you that she's sorry for acting like a big, fat jerk last night," Julia informed him with smile. She wanted her only friend and her boyfriend to get along. *Boyfriend?* That was going to take some getting used to.

"I'm not fat," Melanie scolded her. "Would you guys like to have lunch and go to the zoo today? They are opening a new sea lion exhibit, and I have it on good authority that it's all the rage these days."

Julia giggled, "Good authority, huh? Let me guess, someone passed you the info on a cocktail napkin."

"Yes! How did you know? I thought I was a VIP."

Seth listened to the two friends joke with each other, and it made him miss his friends from his clan. He should have been there to protect them. He should have destroyed Isis when he'd had the chance, so she couldn't have helped the vampire king.

Julia interrupted his thoughts. "She wants us to go to the zoo with her today. How about it?"

"We can do whatever you like," he told her with a forced smile. "But I'd like alone time with you too."

"Ew…Get a room," he heard Melanie say over the phone. Julia laughed and winked at him.

"We are in my room, actually," she replied. "Okay, give us an hour and a half, and we'll meet you outside to take one car. Don't be late."

"Who me? I'm never late." They said their farewells and hung up.

Julia looked at Seth. "Thank you. She's a jerk sometimes, but she is my friend."

"Anything for you. Now, what was that about tipping your waiter?" He asked playfully.

"Well, I did tell her an hour and a half for a reason." She gave him a seductive smile and then her body—including, maybe, a piece of her heart.

Chapter 78

Tressa watched the female vampire storm into the dark Gypsy's house. She had, thankfully, gone unnoticed—she wasn't ready to face the vampires yet. She wanted to do that on her terms and when the time felt right. So, for the moment, she just watched and listened.

Zephryne took Brad by surprise when she shattered his locked front door. "Where are you?" she screamed into the living room.

Brad heard the splintering of wood and then the shrill voice he'd come to loathe and fear. He knew his day of reckoning had arrived when he'd seen the morning news—regrettably, Sasha had failed her mission. He hoped Zephryne remembered that she needed him alive, or his Black Dragon amulet would protect him if she forgot.

"Calm down, Zephryne. Sasha knew the risks. She knew she might have to face off with the Lycan," he called out to her as she made her approach.

"She didn't really understand what a Lycan is! She'd never met one you fool!" She held her clawed hands up like she was ready to spring on him, and she would have if she hadn't heard a clanging sound from the basement. "What's that? Who's down there?" She sniffed the air. "I smell another Gypsy. Is she the one? Is she the one my sister died for?"

Brad was deeply troubled. How would he explain and still get to keep his life, or at the very least his balls, still intact? "No, this is a different woman. She is a strong Gypsy who has passed my test so far. She might actually be the one."

"Run!"

Chapter 79

Brad's side hurt from running through the woods. There was no way he was going to outrun her; she was just toying with him by giving him the head start.

"Zephryne," he hollered, "please stop chasing after me. I didn't mean for her to get killed. I've never come across a Lycan either, so I didn't know how strong they are. I thought Julia was the right Gypsy, and she still might be. There's more than one Gypsy out there, and you need me to wake the prince!"

She easily caught up to him. "Why? You just said yourself that there's more than one Gypsy out there. No one said it had to be *you* to say the spell to wake the prince."

He grasped for straws. "But I'm the descendant of Isis Rosci, who'd cursed the Lycan along with the vampire king two hundred years ago. Therefore, it has to be me."

Zephryne considered his statement. "Perhaps." Then she smiled and knocked him up against a big oak tree.

Brad saw stars then blackness as he lost consciousness, which was not a good state to be in around a hungry vampire.

Chapter 80

Julia lay resting in Seth's arms and began playing with his unusual pendant. "I meant to ask about this earlier, but you were a bad boy and distracted me," she murmured.

Seth pretended to be shocked. "I distracted you? I think you were the seducer today. I'm totally innocent." He batted his lashes at her.

She studied his face and put a fingertip to her chin like she was deep in thought. "You know, I just don't think the jury is going to buy the innocent routine."

"What? You don't think I look innocent?" He puckered his lips in a pout.

"I know you aren't," she chuckled. "Now, back to the necklace, what is it?"

"More or less, it's a good luck charm," he answered.

She turned it over in her palm. "It looks really old, and I've never seen anything like it before. Where did you get it?"

"It's an old family heirloom from my ancestors when they lived in Romania," he told her while looking down at it in her hand.

"Nice. Am I crazy, or did it glow last night?" she wondered.

Seth gave her a wicked grin. "I don't know if I know you well enough to make that determination yet, but, as for the pendant, you may have seen the disco lights bouncing off it."

She smacked his chest playfully. "Well, anyway, I like it. Now, I guess we should get up and shower, so we aren't the late ones." She climbed out of bed and saw his crumpled-up clothes on the floor. "Hey, that's not what you wore last night. Did you leave this morning or something?"

"No, as we were leaving Howl last night, I bumped into someone, and they spilled their drink on me. You fell asleep in the car, so I stopped by my house and changed first." He hated having to lie to her like that.

"Oh, okay. Well, the last one in the shower is a rotten egg!" She took off running, but he caught up to her in two strides, tossed her over his shoulder, and carried her the rest of the way.

"Now nobody has to be a rotten egg," he laughed and gave her a light spank on her bare buttocks.

Playing in the shower led to more lovemaking, which led to them being the late ones after all—by twenty minutes. Surprisingly, Melanie didn't mention it.

During the forty minutes it took for them to get to the zoo, Julia and Melanie told Seth the story of how they'd met when Julia had moved to San Francisco from Colorado eight years ago. He half-heartedly listened, though. It wasn't because he was being rude; it was just because he had only two more nights to make Julia his queen, and then the war would begin, and he would have to somehow keep her safe from it.

Chapter 81

Brad woke up back in his house and wondered if his encounter with Zephryne had just been a dream. Then he heard her cackle and knew that it hadn't been. He was upstairs in his living room, though, while the laughter was coming from the basement. Ofelia was still in the basement. He jumped up from the couch and felt every bone ache in his body. The painful memory of being tossed into the large tree flooded back with a new onslaught of agony, and he wondered if going to the basement was worth the possibility of more pain. *What would Zephryne do to the Gypsy?* She would do nothing because her head would roll, too, if the prince didn't get his queen in time for his coronation as the vampire king. So, if Zephryne wasn't hurting Ofelia, what was the laughter about? He decided he should check it out.

He moved slowly down the stairs and was met with more laughter. "What's so funny? You didn't hurt her, did you? You know what would happen to you…" he stopped mid-sentence as he rounded the corner. "Where is she?"

Brad looked frantically left to right and then up, where he saw the open basement window. Ofelia was gone. But how? She couldn't jump that high to the window, and there was nothing to stand on either. Yet, somehow, she'd escaped—the cunning little bitch. Zephryne was still laughing.

"What do you think is so funny? You have your ass riding on all of this too, or did you forget?" he demanded.

Zephryne stopped laughing and gave him an icy glare. "I know exactly what's riding on all of this, and what

I find so funny is that I don't really need you anymore. You let her go, and now we're both dead, so I should get the pleasure of killing you myself. Don't you think?"

"No, it doesn't have to be over yet. I know where she lives, and we can kill every damn Gypsy in her camp until we flush her out. She won't let that happen. We have two days yet." He backed away from her slowly and pleaded with her while she continued to approach him.

"You idiot!" she hissed. "She's not back at her camp! She's with a witch. I smell a wretched witch."

Chapter 82

Ofelia walked around her new set of confines. She had only a four-foot by four-foot square to pace in because of her shackles. The big boa nearby wouldn't take its beady eyes off her either. She'd been taken captive by a witch, who'd first told her she, too, was Gypsy and that she was there to rescue her from the dark Gypsy, who intended to kill her and make her the bride of the undead. Ofelia already knew about the dark prince, so she'd believed the other woman's story and let her drop a cloth down the wall for her to climb up. But then the woman pulled an athame out on her and bound her wrists. She had forced her back to her cottage by the bay and chained her up where she stood now.

"You are in the way of my plans," the woman, who'd already confessed to being a witch, told her.

Ofelia had no prior dealings with witches, but she'd heard horrible things about them. Then again, before recent events, she'd had no prior dealings with dark Gypsies or vampires either. The witch had taken her amulets away, so she was feeling extra vulnerable. She'd been raised in her camp with the belief that she would do something great for her people one day, but would she still have the chance? She simply had to escape from her new captor.

Tressa watched the young Gypsy pace her small area with pride. It had been so easy to kidnap her from the dark Gypsy. Brad wouldn't know what hit him. That is, if he managed to survive the vampire's wrath.

Pretty Ofelia wouldn't be in her way much longer, though. She knew exactly what she needed to do to secure her own rightful place as the vampire queen. Ofelia didn't want to be the queen to the undead anyway, so really, she was doing the girl a favor. She'd be putting her out of her misery. She would make it as painless as possible for the girl too. Well, except for the cut necessary to spill some of her blood, but the rest would be painless. Tressa could see the whole thing in her mind's eye, and she couldn't wait.

She took a bowl of stew to Ofelia. "Here, you can share my dinner with me." She held the bowl out for the other woman, but Ofelia just stared at it skeptically. "Oh, don't worry, dear. It's not poisoned. See?" She took a bite of it. "You're no use to me dead, at least not yet." There was a squeak nearby, and both women looked down. Tressa stomped on a rat that was scurrying across the room. "Unless you want to have what he's having…" She held the rat to the snake's gaping mouth, and it swallowed the rodent whole.

Ofelia grimaced and turned her head away. What did the witch intend to do to her? And why did the witch and dark Gypsy think she was the destined bride of a vampire? She wasn't a practitioner of dark magic. Her clan was made up of performers and entertainers, who only had good beliefs and practices.

"What do you intend to do to me?" she demanded.

"I suppose I can tell you." The witch cackled and smiled menacingly. "I intend to get rid of you."

"But why? If you are going to kill me, please don't let me die in vain. Tell me why. What did I do to you?"

"You know," Tressa began, "I keep to myself up here in my cottage. I send down random plagues on mankind—a curse here or there just for fun—once in a while, but normally, I leave the world alone and live in solitude. It's just me and my main squeeze, pun intended"—she pointed to the snake—"Then comes along this dark Gypsy, this Brad, and he changes everything. Let me get my bowl of stew, and I'll tell you the whole story."

Chapter 83

"What would you like to look at first?" Seth asked the women.

Julia was the one who answered, "After that episode on the wolf that we watched today, I'd like to look at the wolves."

Seth smiled inside and out. Maybe, just maybe, she'd be more open to the idea of him being a Lycan than he'd thought.

"What are you smiling about?" she asked him.

"I like wolves," he replied with a wink.

Melanie had been studying the park map and pointed north. "The wolves are up that way, so we could walk toward them and just look at the habitats along the way. Then, if we head west, we'll run into the sea lion show and new exhibit."

"Sounds like a good plan to me," Julia said. "Seth, is that okay with you?"

"Whatever makes you happy." He took her hand and led the way, and he was sure he saw Melanie roll her eyes. She would just have to get over it.

The first habitat they stopped at was the bears, which seemed to suddenly become agitated, so a zookeeper had to temporarily close the viewing area off.

"I wonder if someone's perfume set them off," Julia thought aloud.

"That might be," Seth answered, but he knew what it was. They'd smelled a predator.

Along the way, they stopped by the jungle cat exhibit, and the felines roared loudly before trotting inside their cave. When they reached the wolf exhibit, the entire pack came right up to the viewing area, putting a lot of young children in awe. Cameras flashed everywhere as the wolves got up close, and Julia's camera on her phone was no exception.

Suddenly, a man grabbed Melanie's arm and started repeating, "The wolves are coming, and the end will be here. The apocalypse is coming with the blood-red moon. We must protect ourselves and turn to God."

"Get off of me, you crazy loon!" She tried to yank away, but the man wouldn't let go or stop spouting his prophecy.

Seth intervened. He stepped up to the man, and in a calm voice, while the crowd of people observed, told him, "You need to let go of her now." As the man stared into Seth's eyes, Seth pulled his hand loose from Melanie's arm.

The frightened man screamed, "The wolves are here! The wolves are here, and the end is coming," as he ran away from the dumbstruck crowd. Everyone, including Julia, looked at Seth.

"There's someone who has spent too much time in the sun. Let's not let that spoil our adventure." He took Julia's hand again and walked away from the wolves.

"Oh my God, what was that? Melanie are you okay?" Julia was concerned for her friend.

"Yeah, but I'm with you—what was that all about? 'The wolves are here.' Well duh, we were standing right in front of them. He hurt my arm too." She looked down at the bruise already forming and then at Seth. "Thank you for coming to my rescue. How can I repay you?" She batted her lashes when Julia wasn't looking.

"You can just be a great friend to Julia is all," he replied with disinterest, and it seemed to sting her.

Then he looked down at Julia and told her, "If that was you he had grabbed, I would have ripped his arm off. I will do anything to protect you."

Wow. Slow it down. She didn't know how to respond, so she just gave him a weak smile. Sure, she thought of him as her boyfriend, but she wasn't ready to be that serious that fast. She knew she needed to be upfront and tell him, but it would have to wait until they were alone. She didn't want to embarrass him.

Melanie scowled at the back of Julia's head. She had heard what Seth had told her and could only think about how stupid her friend was to take that for granted. Julia never did know a good thing when she had it. Hell, she'd turned down her gorgeous co-worker, Brad, a hundred times for a date. She was just too damned stuck on herself.

She, on the other hand, would be the perfect girl for Seth, and she would love it if he protected her from the big, bad world.

Chapter 84

Tressa explained about Brad's visit to Ofelia. "Lycans? There's another monster I have to worry about now?" the chained-up woman squawked.

"Well, no, not for long," the evil witch smirked. "I'm going to save you from all of that worrying. I'll even make it as painless as possible."

"But why? I don't want to be the vampire queen— you can have it. I just want to go home to my people and be with them when the battle takes place. If I am to die, I want to die with my family," she pleaded from her four by four square.

"That's the problem. Certain people believe that the vampires are your new family, and I just can't have that. I can't have you around if there is the slightest chance that you are the one chosen by the prophets to fulfill the destiny. And if you run, he will find you, and that would be a fate worse than death. Trust that I am saving you from that horrific future"— she looked out the window at the setting sun—"Time is running out." Then she went over to her cauldron and spell books and started working on something that only added to Ofelia's terror.

"Why are you dragging this out then? If you are going to kill me, just do it and get it over with," Ofelia yelped.

"Oh, but it's not the right time yet. It has to be on the eve of the blood moon. That will give me just enough time for my influence to take effect." Tressa smiled and rubbed her fingertip over the blade of the athame she kept in her belt. Then she pricked herself, tasted a drop, and squeezed seven droplets into the cauldron. For pure show, she cackled a witch's infamous cackle.

Chapter 85

Brad looked at Zephryne with a forced smile. "I know where that witch lives."

"And I suppose you're the one who told her about the Gypsy and the vampire prince too," she replied in an agitated tone.

"No, not at all. I only sought her expertise on killing a Lycan. I don't know how she found out about Ofelia, unless she's been following me. That could be it," he explained.

"I don't care how she found out. You get that Gypsy back now or find another to take her place! I'm going to recruit some soldiers for Prince Armando's awakening and for the battle. I'll be back soon, though, to check up on you, so you'd better not let me down. Our new king will hear of all of this when the time is right, so you'd better hope he still finds your services satisfactory, or it will be your neck." She laughed at her pun and then left.

Brad ran back upstairs and pulled out every potion bottle and book he had. He needed strong magic to go up against the witch. There was no other Gypsy to get for the dark prince. True, he hadn't tested Julia, but he wanted her for himself. If he tested her and she passed, then the prince would have her, and if she failed, then no one would have her. It tickled him to think that would also include Seth but hurt his heart to think he couldn't have her then either. It had to be Ofelia. She was strong, and she had bested him. She would make a fine queen for Prince Armando.

Brad mixed together a few potions, which included a sleeping potion, a potion to command someone to do your bidding, and a couple of others to try on the witch. Hopefully, Tressa wasn't stronger than dark Gypsy magic, although, he feared she might be. He might be crazy to go up against her, but there was no other choice. He was dead if he didn't. For good measure, he grabbed what was left of the potion he'd used on Julia. Something had to work out of all that he had. He also grabbed an extra talisman that he'd stolen from a male Gypsy once. It couldn't hurt to take extra fire power.

During his trip across the city to the witch's cottage on the bluffs, he passed by the Longhorn Steakhouse where he'd had his date with Julia, and it panged his heart. Then he saw a yellow car just like hers in the parking lot and came to a screeching halt that was followed by other squealing tires and multiple car horn honks.

He entered the restaurant and looked all around while waving off the hostess, who was trying to seat him. There she was with a dark-haired beauty. His heart skipped a beat, and he started to approach her until a shadow loomed over her table; it was Seth. Of course, considering the day he was having, that Neanderthal would have to be there too.

He was just about to leave and continue his mission when the other woman made eye contact and excused herself from the table. She was headed in his direction with a seductive smile.

Chapter 86

Melanie excused herself when she'd made eye contact with Julia's cute co-worker. Julia shouldn't have all the fun after all.

Julia looked up and saw Melanie walking toward Brad. "Great," she mumbled. "When will that girl learn?" Then another worry crossed her mind—what if he came over to the table and caused a scene? She hoped he had enough common sense not to.

"Hi, you work with Julia Stevens, right? I think I saw you at her firm's Christmas party last year," Melanie said to Brad.

"Yes, I work with her, and I'm sorry, but I'm terrible with names. You are?" He leaned in closer to the attractive woman.

"Melanie. I'm Melanie Conrad." She held out her hand for a shake, but he took it and kissed it instead.

"I don't think Julia introduced us at the party. I know I'd never forget such a lovely lady. I'm Brad Vaughn, by the way."

"Oh, I know who *you* are." She batted her long lashes at him.

"Really? Well, then we should sit down and have a drink and get to know one another better. Can you excuse yourself from their company?" He pointed to Julia and Seth.

She smiled like a Cheshire cat. "I just did." She sat down close to him at the bar.

Julia didn't take her eyes off Melanie and Brad, and Seth followed her stare. "Well, it looks like she has taken up with someone," he observed, knowing that Julia had no idea that he knew just whom she'd taken up with.

"Not just any old someone—he works with me. She's had a crush on him for a long time, and I think he's about to find out."

"What about you?" he fished.

"What about me?" She raised her eyebrows and cocked her head.

"Have you ever had a crush on him?" He held his breath while waiting for her answer.

Julia was sure her face turned red. It would be from shame, though, not embarrassment. "No, and I don't date co-workers even if I did."

Seth smiled in relief. "Well, that is good to know because I thought about applying for a job at your firm, so I could spend more time with you."

"And do you know anything about doing corporate and personal taxes?" she played along.

"No, but I was hoping to be your personal assistant," he replied with a wink.

"Well, I have one of those already, and she's quite good and wouldn't hesitate to fight you for her job," she laughed.

"So, it's a woman. Good. I would hate to hear that the boy next door over there is your assistant."

"Oh please," she groaned and rolled her eyes. "Like you would have anything to worry about."

"So, you think I'm cute then?" He reached across the table and ran his fingertips lightly over the back of her hand.

"Yeah, I think you're pretty easy on the eyes," she purred.

"Awe, shucks." He looked down, feigning embarrassment. "I think you're drop-dead gorgeous, my lady." He nodded toward Melanie and Brad, who were deep in conversation. "Have you ever thought about fixing them up?"

"No, absolutely not. I don't want to create an uncomfortable work environment." *Even though I just did.* "Besides, Melanie doesn't have a good track record with men." She watched the two of them chatting. If he told Melanie about their afternoon in his bed, she'd kill him. "I'm finished, are you ready to go? He can always drive her home if she doesn't want to come with us," she suggested.

"Yes, let's get out of here, and I think it's safer if she just comes with us. There's a serial killer still on the loose," he commented.

She shot him a hard look. "Well, it isn't Brad!"

"How do you know that, Julia? How well do you really know him?" he questioned, and she could tell by his tone that he was serious.

She felt flustered, and her voice came out high-pitched. "I know him better than I know you, and I don't think you're the killer either. Don't worry about her, Seth. It's not Brad, and she'll be fine."

Seth didn't know what else he could say. He may not care for Julia's friend, but he didn't want to see her get hurt either. He looked down at his hands and noticed that the pendant was glowing under his black T-shirt. He stood up quickly, hoping that Julia wouldn't see it.

"Fine, but I don't want you alone with him—ever," he grumbled.

Julia just stared with her mouth open, but no words came out. He was behaving outlandish and possessive again. She really needed to talk to him about it.

Melanie had treated them to dinner as part of her apology and to thank Seth for saving her from the crazy guy at the zoo, so they could just leave. They stopped by her and Brad on the way out, though.

"We're ready to go, so are you coming with us, or do you want to find your own way back?" Julia asked her.

Brad spoke for Melanie, "Don't worry, Julia, I'll make sure Little Red Riding Hood gets home without being eaten by the big, bad wolf. This must be Seth." Brad extended his hand to the Lycan. He was sure the amulet would protect him, just as it had the first time they'd crossed paths.

Seth took the man's hand and squeezed—hard.

"Wow," Brad gasped and yanked his arm back. "You've got quite the grip, big guy."

Julia looked down and saw that Brad's hand was red, and then she looked up at Seth who was giving the man a stare that was full of daggers. She couldn't help but wonder what it was all about. On the plus side, she doubted Brad would ever spill the beans about them now.

"Well, good night then. Have fun," she told them. "Brad, I guess I'll see you at work tomorrow, and, Melanie, I'll call you later."

As they left, she was sure Seth bumped into Brad on purpose. *What is that all about?*

Chapter 87

In the car on the way back to her place, she decided to interrogate him. "What was that all about? Do you have something against Brad? I mean, why would you think he's a serial killer?"

"If you want the honest truth, I just don't trust him. I saw the way he looks at you, and I recognize that look. He's interested in you, Julia."

He didn't even try to disguise the disdain in his voice. If only he could tell her who Brad really was. If only he could explain that Brad was the one who was killing Gypsies. But he'd just left her friend with the man, so he couldn't admit to knowing full-well who the creep was. He would just have to take care of him before he could hurt anyone else and hope that he didn't hurt Melanie in the meantime.

The rest of the drive was quiet, and tension filled the car. Then at a stop sign, a man, who was dressed in tattered clothing and holding up a sign, ran out in front of the car, and Julia had to slam on the brakes to avoid hitting him.

She honked the horn and rolled down her window to shout, "Are you insane? I almost hit you!"

"It's coming! The end of the world is coming! We must pray!" he shouted the same thing that was written on his sign. Strangely, it wasn't even the same man from the zoo.

"That's crazy"—she tossed a glance at Seth— "What is going on with people today?"

He answered in a solemn tone, "They're just afraid of the blood moon that's coming." *And they should be.*

"Why does everyone seem to think that the blood moon has a religious connection? I think it's just scientific—a natural phenomenon. Do you think it has a special meaning or purpose?" she wondered.

She had just parked the car in the parking lot at her apartment building, and before exiting the vehicle, he looked at her and gravely answered, "Yes, I sure do."

Chapter 88

Brad took Melanie back to his house, thinking that after he drove her home later, he would go after Ofelia. He figured it might be easier to surprise the witch at night. Then again, he also considered the fact that it would be scarier for him too. Oh well, he was going to enjoy the hot little number if it was the last thing he'd do.

They were kissing, and she clutched at his shirt, trying to pull it off him. He pushed her hand away and removed it himself. Her eyes went right to the amulets he wore and went wide at the sight of the Black Dragon.

"How did you get that? How do you have the Black Dragon amulet?" She stepped backward and stared at it.

"How do you know about the Black Dragon? It's my family heirloom, and no one else knows about it." His voice was shrill when he demanded her answer.

Melanie continued to stare at it. "I don't know for sure, but I know I've seen it somewhere before. Let me think." She put her fingers to her temples and rubbed while she closed her eyes and concentrated. "I can't remember, but I recognize it. This is going to drive me nuts trying to remember."

"I think I can help you recall. Do you trust me?" he asked while digging in a drawer for something.

"I guess so," she answered with a modicum of hesitation.

Brad produced a crystal pendulum and a bottle of liquid from the drawer. He used the dropper from the decanter to put two drops of a blue substance onto the crystal. Then he swung the pendulum back and forth in front of her while chanting something from a piece of script paper that he held in his other hand.

"Uite în interiorul mintea lui ochi pentru a vedea ce secrete se află adânc. Găsi răspunsul vreau ei de a oferi pentru mine." *Look inside the mind's eye to see what secret lies deep. Find the answer I want her to provide for me.* After two repetitions, she focused her eyes on his.

"I can remember! I saw it once before at my grandmother's house when I was a child. I found it in her jewelry box. She was angry with me at first, but then she sat me down and told me what it was and that it belonged to our family. She said that it would be mine one day." She looked at the amulet again and softly added, "How do you have *my* family's heirloom? Did you steal it?"

Brad could tell she was afraid of him and quite confused. He was confused too. The Black Dragon had never left his family's possession, not even for one second. He'd been raised around it and had watched it be passed down from his great grandfather, to his grandmother, to his mother, and finally to him. Her story made no sense at all. Each generation bore but one child, so he didn't have siblings or cousins on his mother's side.

"Come in here with me," he commanded her as he walked into his study.

Melanie followed him without a word—she was too afraid to speak.

Brad grabbed the book of Rosci off its place on the bookshelf inside a hidden cabinet. Melanie watched and saw the title.

"Wait! Rosci was my grandmother's name when she was a baby. She was born Isabel Rosci but was adopted by Geoffrey and Thelma Clark, my great-grandparents, who couldn't have children. Then grandmother married Phillip Conrad and had my father, Phillip Conrad II."

Brad found what he had been searching for in the book while she told him her story. His great-grandmother bore a set of twin girls but one of the babes had died at birth. That was the only instance where more than one child had been born, which was to keep the family line strong. It was better to keep the family's power concentrated in a few individuals than to spread it thin among many. It is also why his mother raised him without a father in the picture. She had wanted the magic to be strong in Brad.

"What? What are you reading? Did you find something?" she demanded, overcoming her fear.

He looked at her with crazed eyes. "There were twins, but one died—only she didn't. She didn't die; she was your grandmother, my grandmother's sister. That makes my grandmother your father's aunt and your father and my mother cousins. So, that means we are third cousins."

"Ew, gross! I was making out with my cousin?" She made a horrified face.

"Oh, calm down. It's legal for third cousins to marry. The bigger issue here is this—do you have any idea who you are?" He held up the Black Dragon. "Do you even know what this represents?"

Melanie blinked her eyes rapidly. "No, I just remembered seeing it before at my grandmother's. So, you still haven't said how you got it, cousin." She crossed her arms over her chest and waited for his answer.

"There must have been two. They must have given one to each girl for protection," he surmised.

"Protection from what, and what does it do?" She was growing impatient with his cryptic answers.

Brad looked out the window at the full moon. "Sit down, Melanie. We have a lot to cover and not much time. You need to know about your heritage and your destiny as part of the Rosci clan."

Chapter 89

"Well, what does that mean?" Julia asked. "What do you think it means then?"

Seth sniffed the air to be sure no vampires had come back around and then patiently answered her, "I will explain everything when we are inside, and I have your undivided attention."

"Why are you smelling the air? I've seen you do that before," she pressed.

"Again," he answered her softly, "I'll explain everything when we are inside."

Oscar was happy to see them, and they leashed him up for his walk. As soon as they stepped back outside, though, the dog began to growl, and Seth took off running for the woods.

"Get inside now!" he yelled over his shoulder, and Oscar yanked hard toward the door. Julia stood her ground, though, and couldn't believe what she was witnessing. Seth was throwing his clothes onto the ground while he ran, and then he leapt into the air and disappeared into the trees.

"What the hell?" Julia exclaimed. She couldn't believe her eyes, and Oscar was right up against her still growling and pulling her toward the building door. "Okay, have it your way. Hold it in then," she snapped and took the fierce dog back upstairs.

She had no idea what all was going on, but she was going to demand an explanation when and if she saw Seth again. First, there was the weird stuff at the zoo, then his reaction to Brad, then the crazy guy on the way home, which led to the talk of the blood moon, and then him running into the woods again. Maybe the full moon was making everyone crazy. She thought of her own behavior at Brad's house; maybe she should just blame that on the moon too.

Chapter 90

Zephryne ran through the woods as fast as she could. She'd been out hunting more prey when she stumbled back upon the mortal's building. It figured that the Lycan was there, and that it had smelled her. It was chasing her through the forest, intending to slaughter her the way it did her poor sister.

Seth raced after the vampire, determined to catch her. He wondered how many more were around too. They were probably preparing an army for the vampire prince, so it was hard to guess how many blood suckers were running around. He needed to tell Julia the truth, and he needed to do it before the night was over. He continued to run for five more miles and then circled back. The vampire was gone, and he needed to go back to Julia's to protect her and tell her the truth—if only he could protect her from that.

It was twenty minutes before he got back to her building. Out of breath, he re-dressed and headed up her stairs with a worried heart. How in the world was he going to pull this off? Then the pendant of λύκος did something it hadn't done before—it grew warm, as if it was really trying to get his attention. It worked. He held the scalding pendant, and the answer came to him. He'd first use the necklace's powers to show her the truth, and then he'd enlist Madame Elmira's help in the morning. Then he remembered something the Gypsy had told him. She'd told him that he was the keeper of the answers—they were with him all along. She must have meant the necklace. The pendant of λύκος knew what to do and held the power all along.

He knocked lightly on her apartment door and called out, "Julia, it's Seth. Will you let me in, so I can explain, please?" He could hear Oscar whine and paw at the door. Finally, the lock clicked, and the door opened.

"I'm only letting you in because Oscar asked me to, and he is usually a good judge of character," she declared without making eye contact. Then she looked up into his face and shouted, "Now what the hell is going on?"

"I understand that you have questions, and I'm ready to tell you everything," he began.

"*Everything?* How much is there? How many secrets do you have?" she demanded.

"It's quite a bit to absorb, so please sit on the couch with me." He led the way to her sofa, and they both sat down. Seth tried to take her hand in his, but she pulled away. *This isn't going to be easy even with magical jewelry.* He began his explanation, "If you remember, I told you that my family came here from Romania. Well, that was slightly over two hundred years ago. Times were so different back then. The land was raw and full of barbarity, men and"— he looked down at his hands—"monsters who were fighting for it."

"Where are you going with this? Are you giving me a history lesson or an answer?" she squawked.

"Actually, they go hand in hand, and the easiest way for me to explain everything is to just show you." He fondled his pendant while staring into her eyes.

"Show me? How are you going to show me?" she questioned.

"You asked about my pendant," he said while removing it. "Well, what I told you is true, but what you don't know is that it's magical too."

"Oh Lord!" She rolled her eyes. "Are we back to Gypsies and fortune tellers and stuff like that again?"

He could tell she was getting irritated, and he needed to speed the process up. "Yes, we are. Here"—he thrust it toward her—"I need you to hold it." He cupped the pendant in her hands and told it, in his language, to show her. Then he watched as her body jerked and trembled while she was shown everything.

Julia's eyes flew back open, and she stared at him, speechless at first. "What kind of trick is this? How did you do that? Am I hypnotized or something? I don't understand." Her arms flailed while she spoke, and the necklace fell to the floor.

"No, it's not a trick. It's very real," he replied while picking it back up and clasping it around his neck.

Julia jumped up from the couch and shouted, "Then you're a monster? You're a werewolf? You killed James"—she backed away from him—"and what about Brad? You knew about him, but you didn't tell me! You let Melanie go with him! I have to call her." She ran to get her phone from her purse, but she didn't run out the door.

"I'm not a werewolf, I'm a Lycan, but you shouldn't be afraid. I'm not going to hurt you, and I feel bad that I had to destroy the hunter."

"Oh really? Apparently, you felt bad enough to drug me, so I'd forget his house. Forget about calling Melanie; I should call the damn cops."

He took the phone from her hands, though. "That would do you no good. I'll stop Brad, and I'll stop the vampires too."

"Oh God, *vampires?* Yes, let's talk about that, shall we? I'm being informed that there are evil Gypsies, werewolves, witches, and vampires that really exist among us. Did I leave anyone out?" She shook her head. "How am I supposed to believe any of this? It's just preposterous!"

"I can show you," he told her softly.

"What, with more jewelry? Are your shoes magical and going to tell me something else? Am I on candid camera?" she ranted.

"No, like this." He undressed and shifted.

Julia screamed loud enough to wake the dead, and a neighbor came pounding on her door. "Are you okay? Should I call the police?" the elderly man called out to her.

"No, everything is okay. I just saw a huge spider," she replied, and after taking a good look at the gigantic monster in her living room, she fainted.

Chapter 91

April 14, 2014

The morning sun hit Julia's face, and she sat up in bed with a start. Seth was sound asleep next to her, and Oscar was at the foot of the bed like usual. *Whew! It was all just a bad dream.* But it hadn't felt like a dream, had it? She was completely lucid when Seth confessed and showed her things that blew her mind. But, still, that couldn't be real. Feeling silly, she reached out and took ahold of his pendant, and the tidal wave of truth consumed her once more. She shrieked, and Seth's eyes flew open.

"What? What's wrong?" He tried to pull her into the shelter of his body, but she yanked away from him.

"If all this is true, then everything is wrong. You're a Lycan, Brad is a serial killer, and the world is going to end, and you think I can stop it if I help you somehow. That's what's wrong!" Tears spilled down her cheeks, and her body quaked.

"No, my love, it won't end like that. I'll stop the vampires with my Lycan army—the one you'll help me build. Together, we'll forge a strength that will overcome anything and will stop the apocalypse. It will all be okay. I promise you that I won't let anything bad happen to you. You're destined to be my queen."

"How can I make an army with you? And I've barely accepted having a boyfriend, but you're talking about getting married—*right now*. I already thought you were moving too fast for me, but this is nuts. I'm not marriage material, and I'm not a Lycan."

"You don't have to be. You'll be my queen and bare my young, and the Lycans who are still out there will pledge their allegiance to us, while others will join us by becoming Lycan if they choose. I won't force anyone. Now today, we'll go see Madame Elmira to see if there is anything else we must do before tomorrow's blood moon."

"What about Melanie?" she whispered with concern in her voice and eyes.

"Call her and see if she's okay," he advised and patted her hand.

"Okay, but I have to call into work first." She grabbed her phone and left a message on the office answering machine that she was going to take a couple of days off for personal reasons.

Brad was standing there as the message was left, and he couldn't help but wonder what her reasons were. He wondered if she knew the Lycan's plans for her, and if she also found out who he really was. *Do you have any idea what my plans are for you?* Perhaps he would send her dear friend Melanie to find out. It was time Melanie earned her place in the family tree anyway. It was time for them to act.

Chapter 92

Julia tried Melanie's number, but it went to voicemail after two rings, which probably meant that she was on another call, so she'd have to try again in a little while. She and Seth got ready to go see Madame Elmira after taking Oscar out for his morning walk.

The visit with the Gypsy didn't do much to clarify things for Julia, though. She just repeated things Seth had already told her and what the pendant had shown her. But she was concerned about something; Julia could read it on the woman's face.

"What aren't you saying?" Julia asked.

"I was wondering the same thing," Seth chimed in.

The Gypsy wrung her hands together before meeting their gazes. "I don't know if I'm being foolish, but I don't think Julia is the one. I don't think she's the Gypsy who is the key."

"I'm not a Gypsy," Julia answered. "Did I miss something when you said I'm your queen?" She stared at Seth in confusion.

He looked confused as well. "But the pendant showed her the truth, and it wouldn't have worked if she wasn't intended to learn from it."

"Let me explain myself and what I'm thinking. I don't doubt that Julia is to be your queen. She is the only who has ever captured your heart, and as you have already said, your pendant worked for her. But I don't think she's the key to the battle being won." She flipped three tarot cards over. "I see two more forces out there that are somehow involved. You have until tomorrow night to figure out who or what they are. That is all I can give you at this point. I've been studying the books and star charts, and I keep coming up to the number three. They're like points of a triangle, and they all point to you, Seth. Let your pendant continue to guide you to the answers. Now go. You have little time to be prepared. Tomorrow begins the next chapter of life—for us all."

On the way back to Julia's apartment, she tried Melanie again. This time her friend answered, and she assured Julia that she had a wonderful time with Brad and had made it home safe and sound.

"It was like catching up with an old friend," Melanie told her. "Is there anything new with you?"

"No," Julia responded and then told her friend good-bye.

Chapter 93

"It's time for you to play your part, Ofelia." Tressa drank the vial of potion she'd made the night before, and then she used her athame to cut Ofelia's wrist. She drew the Gypsy's wrist up to her mouth and sipped her blood. She almost spat the salty fluid out, though. "I guess it's an acquired taste," she told the cringing woman. "Oh, lighten up. This will all be over with before you know it. At least for you it will be," she laughed and looked out the window at the bay, smiling.

"What are you going to do to me?" Ofelia asked, trying to remain brave in the face of death.

"You'll find out soon enough, my dear. You'll find out soon enough," she repeated just as there was a knock on her front door. "Hmm…now I wonder who on earth that could be. Care to place your bets? I bet it's the dark Gypsy, and he wants to steal you back. What do you think?"

"I don't know, but I hope it's Dorothy from the freaking Wizard of Oz with a big bucket of water," Ofelia spat at her.

Tressa roared with laughter. "That's a good one. Good for you, making jokes before you die." She walked off to get the door, and, of course, it was Brad, but he wasn't alone. There was a young woman with him this time. "What's this? Did you bring a friend to see me this time?"

"Even better, witch. I brought another Rosci this time. We are here to take back the Gypsy, and I know you have her. I don't know why you have her, but she's coming with us."

"Brad, you're such a fool. That Gypsy isn't the powerful one meant to be the bride of the dark prince; I am. It's my power he seeks from beyond his sleep, and it's my power that will help him raise his army and defeat the Lycans. I'm the one who will make him the king of the vampires. I'm his true queen."

"That's not true, witch. I've seen her power, and it's strong Gypsy magic."

"Again, you're such a fool. Or is naive a better term for you? Either way, I dipped your amulet in a power stripping potion. She didn't best you, I did. She might be cunning and strong-willed, but I am the most powerful Gypsy. That's right, I said Gypsy." She looked Melanie up and down while Brad stood there gaping. "And what is it you want out of this? Do you want to be queen too? Were you just going to kill poor Ofelia and take the throne with the dark prince yourself? I can read it on your face, darling. You need to learn how to play poker," she chuckled.

"I've no interest in being the vampire bride. I only wish to see the Lycan suffer for what he's done to me and our ancestor." She tossed a glance at Brad.

"Your ancestor? Do you mean Isis Rosci by chance? Yes, I know all about her and Brad's path for revenge. I know she was the one who cursed the Lycan into eternal sleep, but we see how well that magic worked, don't we? Your family's magic isn't enough, children. You'll need mine too. We all want the same thing here—for the vampire king to reign and his army of the undead to defeat the Lycans and send them to the bowels of hell once and for all. And, of course, there's King Seth's mortal love to deal with."

"No! She's mine. I want her for myself," Brad roared and widened his stance.

"Fine, have the little wench. She doesn't concern me," Tressa told him. Then she looked at Melanie. "And the Lycan bride? You wish for that to be you, don't you? You want to complete the path Isis had been on. You want what she wasn't able to achieve—his love."

"No, I will not side with the Lycans. But I do want him to suffer and Julia too," she answered with a malicious smile.

"So, we agree then? We will work together to fulfill the vampire prince's destiny and be rewarded under his reign." Tressa studied both of them for their compliance.

"Yes, we are agreed then," Brad replied, and Melanie nodded. "Now what about her?" He pointed to the corner of the room where Ofelia stood.

"Well, she is about to do a swan dive. Would you like to watch?" Tressa hissed with an evil smile.

"Oh yes," they both eagerly agreed.

Chapter 94

Julia and Seth were taking in a late afternoon picnic in a secluded area of the bay. They wanted to spend as much time enjoying each other's company before all hell broke loose. Julia accepted him for what he was, and she was working on accepting what everything about to happen could mean for her, for them, and for the world.

She hadn't talked much with Melanie, who suddenly didn't want to return her calls or stay on the line with her for more than twenty seconds at a time, but she did warn her friend to stay away from Brad. She couldn't very well tell Melanie the truth, so she lied and said she knew for a fact that he had a girlfriend because she kept coming up to his office. Melanie responded that it didn't matter because she was moving on to bigger and better things anyway.

Julia sat with Seth on the sand and watched a couple of dolphins splashing around in the ocean when the pendant of λύκος began to glow. "What does that mean? Why is it doing that?"

Seth looked down and fingered the pendant. "It means I'm where I'm supposed to be." He looked around them. "Something is about to happen." Then they both heard a woman's scream and looked up frantically to see a body falling from the bluffs to their east. Seth broke into a run across the sand and dove into the water just as the sun began to set.

Julia waited for what seemed like forever before he was back with the woman who'd fallen from the bluffs.

Julia began CPR on the frail woman, and, all the while, Seth's pendant glowed.

Ofelia felt water rising up her throat and turned her head to cough out the salty ocean as fresh air rushed into her burning lungs. Her eyes slowly fluttered open to see the face of her heroes.

"Can you get me home to my camp by Chinatown? I was abducted a few days ago, and I know my family is worried sick." Her voice was hoarse from coughing.

Seth studied the young woman and processed her words. "Are you a Gypsy?"

"Yes, I am Romani," the woman replied.

"We will certainly help you. Your people have been good to me," he informed her.

He helped both her and Julia up off the sand and drove them to Chinatown, where she was greeted with several pairs of teary eyes. One set of eyes actually belonged to Madame Elmira, who turned out to be the woman's aunt.

"My prayers have been answered! You found and saved my precious niece, Ofelia." She tightly embraced the young Gypsy. "I told you to follow your pendant, and it would lead you where you need to go," she talked excitedly. "This must mean my Ophelia is the one. She is the destined one. She is the second point in the triangle."

"I don't understand," Seth remarked.

"Yes, I don't either," Ofelia agreed and looked at her aunt, then Seth, and then Julia, who wasn't saying anything.

"Let's all sit down and talk," Madame Elmira addressed the camp.

She explained to the camp everything that had happened the last several days and what her muddled vision had been telling her all along—that a powerful Gypsy would rise up and help the Lycans defeat the vampires. She told them that Ofelia was that destined

Gypsy. She would gather her people under her leadership, and they would fight side by side with the Lycan army.

Everyone looked up at the sky—they had a long night of planning ahead. But first, underneath the waxing gibbous, they had a wedding—Seth and Julia's. The long-lost king of the Lycans finally claimed his queen, and he did it just in time.

Chapter 95

April 15, 2014
Night of the Blood Moon

After a few spoken words, some spilled blood, and a thousand years of lying in wait, black eyes opened to the coming of night. The vampire prince, Prince Armando, rose from his crypt and greeted his followers. Brad, Melanie, and Tressa were among them.

Zephryne approached him first. "Good evening, my future king. I have prepared a small army for your arrival, and we have your bride here as well to complete the prophecy." She turned to Tressa and said, "Come forth witch."

"Witch?" he growled, "I do not recall there being a witch in the prophecy I was foretold before my rest."

"I am a dark Gypsy, who turned to witchcraft to harness my power," Tressa stated and stepped forth. "My power combined with yours, of course, will tear down the Lycan army and sweep across the world in a plague." She gave him a vindictive smile.

"So, the Lycans have fulfilled their end of the prophecy as well? The king is awake and has found his queen?"

Tressa was the one who answered because Brad was too nervous to speak. "Yes, the king is awake, but I'm sure he will be no match for you—for us. I do not know if he has found his queen or not. The only good Gypsy strong enough to be queen is now fish food. The dark Gypsy"—she pointed to Brad—"was going to bring her here for you, but I knew she would never suffice. I am the only one strong enough to carry out your wishes, my lord." She bowed before him. "Now, shall we say our dark vows and anoint you King Armando?"

He smiled at the pretty witch. "Yes, but I'm famished." He grabbed Tressa's arm and pulled her into his iron embrace while he sank his fangs into the soft skin on her neck. He drained her completely while the others watched and then let her body sink to the ground. "Get rid of the cocky bitch," he told Zephryne. Then he turned to Brad and said, "I don't doubt that you have found a suitable queen for me."

"But the witch killed her, my lord," Brad stuttered and nervously shuffled his feet.

"No, she's right here." The dark prince looked squarely at Melanie.

Turn the page for a preview of Birthright

ONE

1601 Transylvania

Red eyes peeked through the cover of trees. The prey stood not more than twenty yards away. He could see its breath swirling around its nostrils in the early-evening fog, and he could hear it snorting with its heavy breathing as it pawed the earth. Just another second or two and he'd make his move. He reared back on his haunches and broke through the brush at sixty-five miles per hour before pouncing. In a split second, he was on top of the writhing buck, biting into the animal's thick neck. He tore its throat out and began feasting on the warm salty flesh.

Not far from the smorgasbord, a couple embraced nature's guilty pleasure on the green grass. Their naked bodies entwined under the rolling fog, and soft moans of enjoyment echoed off the hillside. Their sounds of lovemaking drowned out the sounds of flesh being torn from bone only a matter of feet away from them.

Damian tossed the naked wench onto her back and buried his face between her taut quivering thighs. He would've preferred to take his time with the woman, but he felt starved. He licked, nibbled, and sucked on her thigh until she ran wet, writhed, and screamed for more. To answer her cries, he used his fingers to pleasure her while his other hand ran its nails down her wriggling leg. He could tell she was about to explode from her lust for him; he could feel it all around his finger, see it on her face, and hear it in her cries. His own need grew strong as well, and it wasn't just the one pulsing solid and steady between his muscular thighs. His thirst needed to be fed too. His razor-sharp fangs involuntarily elongated in response to the thought, and he ran his tongue over them. The woman's eyes were half closed from desire, so she didn't notice the change, which was good because he wasn't in the mood for a struggle. He rose to his knees and put her ankles on his massive shoulders. Then, as he forced himself inside her welcoming passage, he bit shallowly into her ankle and began to suckle her warm blood. Her life's force filled his greedy mouth, and its metallic scent his nostrils while her body thrashed in pleasure from his slow, steady strokes. As his energy was replenished, his tempo picked up, and he pulled away from her petite ankle to push her knees into her chest and pressed his body down on them. His girth filled her even deeper, and she squealed in delight. He grunted from his own enjoyment and then took a rosy bud into his hungry mouth. While suckling the taut peak, he pinned her wrists above her head, which seemed to arouse her more, and then he ran the tip of his tongue from her wet nipple up the mound and to her long luscious neck. He pressed gentle kisses around her pulse at first, playing with the rhythmic beat of her heart. Its steady throbbing called to him like a siren's song, and he answered by sinking his fangs into her delicate flesh. Luckily for her, his saliva contained a numbing agent, so she didn't feel much more than a playful nip. He fed his thirst with long pulls on her salty blood while his clawed hand kneaded her breast. The other still had her wrists pinned just in case she got feisty. She didn't struggle, though; she just moved metrically with each stroke he gave her and rode wave after wave of pleasure. He could feel her climaxes around his shaft squeezing and pulling him toward his own release. Then she stopped moving with him, and her chest ceased to rise and fall. As her last breath escaped her lips on a sigh, his culmination was upon him, and he filled her corpse with his heated lust.

Necrophilia? Maybe so. He chuckled softly to himself and rolled away from her lifeless body while licking the last droplet from his perfect lips. *Waste not, want not.*

He looked over at the woman with an ounce of pity and traced a nail down her bare chest. She was his second woman for the day—there had been breakfast too.

An exasperated sigh sounded from behind him followed by, "Are you done yet?" Logan, his brother, was always the impatient one, but that was probably the wolf in him.

"Yes, I'm done, and I don't interrupt *you* during dinner."

"Well, I don't play with my food the way you do"—he squinted his eyes in thought—"At least not always." A lopsided grin adorned his handsome face, and he tilted his head until his thick neck popped once on each side. "I'm bored. Can we go now?"

Damian looked around the tree line where they were. The question was, go where? There were three unknowns. They didn't know who'd killed their mother and abducted their father, they didn't know where to look for him, and they didn't know why war was waged, but they did know one thing for certain—someone would pay.

Now, he looked up at the sky and the setting sun, casting shades of pinks, oranges, and purples across the quickly darkening canvas, and grunted, "North."

"How far are we traveling tonight?"

Damian sighed deeply before answering his younger brother by all of two minutes. "We'll travel into Brasov and talk to the townsfolk in the sunup. Someone there has to have seen something." He led the way, and Logan followed right behind him.

"Do you think they'll talk to us? We aren't exactly known to them," Logan pointed out.

Damian slanted his eyes, grinned a toothy grin, and growled, "We'll make them talk."

Logan chuckled low in his throat and extended his claws, which he then swiped at the air. "Yeah, we will," he eagerly agreed.

If Lucian Dragovich, their father, was around, he'd order them to act dignified when in the presence of the townspeople because they were, in his eyes, still royalty even if the villagers no longer recognized the kingdom of Drago. When Lucian's father, King Titus, died, the throne died along with him. Lucian was too young to take it over, and his mother had already died years before. Mortality, unfortunately, was not a stranger to their breed. It is true, though, that the aging process remarkably slowed when maturity was reached around the age of twenty years.

They learned through research that vampires stopped aging altogether at about age thirty, but that didn't guarantee them an immortal existence either. This they knew from personal experience since much vampire blood was shed in the rescuing of Damian when he was two. To date, the twins were healthy, fully-fleshed twenty-one-year-olds with appetites for adventure, danger, sex, and revenge.

When the fraternal twins had been born, the chance for a rebirth of the kingdom had become possible since Lucian could, no doubt, stand strong with his two werewolf sons beside him at the throne. Hope had even sparked in the villages surrounding Drago until the vampires had kidnapped Damian, causing the embers to die down. When he had been safely rescued—but it had become evident that he had been turned into a vampire—the embers burned out altogether. Of the "immortals," vampires were the most feared—they were not at all trusted by the townspeople. One too many babe and maiden had been snatched away in the night by a blood-thirsty vampire.

While Damian was still accepted as Lucian's son, he was never looked upon or treated quite the same as Logan by the villagers. Then, when Lucian's boys had entered their teen years, the villagers side-stepped both of them when they were seen coming. However, it was for different reasons. Logan was mostly avoided because he was a shit-disturber and made trouble everywhere he went. Damian was simply feared. The werewolf-turned-vampire was the first of his kind, and no one knew what to expect from him. He didn't even know what to expect with the passing of time. But of course, at the moment, he had bigger things to worry about.

Logan must have read his mind because he suddenly blurted out, "What if they don't know?"

Damian drew a hand across his dark chiseled features in thought. "Someone knows."

"When do you want to take our rest?"

Damian could hear the fatigue in his brother's voice, and the truth was he was feeling it himself, so he replied, "Here. We'll stop here till sunup."

He removed his belted sword, tossed it to the ground, and then lay down on the soft earth. In their hurry, they'd grabbed their weapons and only a few wares to sustain themselves on their journey. In a sack, he'd thrown some dried salt pork and bread—blood wasn't the only food he consumed, although it was the most important and the tastiest. After his rescue, though, his father had made a promise to the nearby communities, when it became clear what Damian was. He'd promised that Damian would only feed upon the dying. He would be the Angel of Death and help them transition to the other side. And so it became an unwritten law. That is until Damian grew older and curious, and he started sneaking off to find lively prey on his own. That was also when he'd discovered the pleasures of women.

"Damian?" Logan's voice was hoarse with emotion, and it scared off some nearby wildlife.

"What is it?"

"I'm going to miss her," he answered softly this time, and Damian could hear him struggling with tears. A display of weakness, for any reason, was not acceptable behavior for a werewolf and especially not for the son of a king.

"Aye, me too," Damian grunted. "Get some sleep. We don't have long." Fortunately, they didn't need long. They only needed a couple of hours of rest each night to be able to maintain their stamina.

Loud snoring sounded from Logan's direction to announce his departure to the dream realm, and Damian smiled to himself thinking that maybe he'd see their mother there. Maybe they both would. He closed his eyes and drifted off too.

His dreams were fitful, though. He was taken back to the castle, to the moment when Logan and he knew something was wrong. It was too quiet, and then they spotted the blood. It was just a little at first, but the trail took them to bigger pools and finally to their mother's cold body.

Damian bolted upright hissing with his fangs showing, which caused Logan to jump to all fours, in pouncing position, with his fangs bared as well.

"Where?" Logan growled.

"Nowhere—it was just a bad dream," Damian admitted and felt foolish.

Logan stood up and popped his neck on both sides. "Well, since we are both awake anyway, I say we keep going. Brasov isn't too far from here."

Damian looked at the moon still hanging low in the sky. "Aye, let's keep going then." They grabbed their meager belongings and continued to tread northbound to the small village.